Mind Over Murder

"A delightful read . . . [A] winning addition to the cozy paranormal mystery realm."
—Yasmine Galenorn, *New York Times* bestselling author

"The breakout must-read mystery of the fall season. [It] is a definite contender for best new cozy series of 2011 . . . Kingsley's inhabitants are a sensational cast of players with exhilarating and quirky personalities that vibrantly jump off the page, engaging the reader immediately."
—*Seattle Post-Intelligencer*

Berkley Prime Crime titles by Allison Kingsley

MIND OVER MURDER
A SINISTER SENSE

A Sinister Sense

Allison Kingsley

BERKLEY PRIME CRIME, NEW YORK

THE BERKLEY PUBLISHING GROUP
Published by the Penguin Group
Penguin Group (USA) Inc.
375 Hudson Street, New York, New York 10014, USA

Penguin Group (Canada), 90 Eglinton Avenue East, Suite 700, Toronto, Ontario M4P 2Y3, Canada (a division of Pearson Penguin Canada Inc.) • Penguin Books Ltd., 80 Strand, London WC2R 0RL, England • Penguin Group Ireland, 25 St. Stephen's Green, Dublin 2, Ireland (a division of Penguin Books Ltd.) • Penguin Group (Australia), 250 Camberwell Road, Camberwell, Victoria 3124, Australia (a division of Pearson Australia Group Pty. Ltd.) • Penguin Books India Pvt. Ltd., 11 Community Centre, Panchsheel Park, New Delhi—110 017, India • Penguin Group (NZ), 67 Apollo Drive, Rosedale, Auckland 0632, New Zealand (a division of Pearson New Zealand Ltd.) • Penguin Books (South Africa) (Pty.) Ltd., 24 Sturdee Avenue, Rosebank, Johannesburg 2196, South Africa

Penguin Books Ltd., Registered Offices: 80 Strand, London WC2R 0RL, England

A SINISTER SENSE

A Berkley Prime Crime Book / published by arrangement with the author

PUBLISHING HISTORY
Berkley Prime Crime mass-market edition / July 2012

Copyright © 2012 by Penguin Group (USA) Inc.
Cover illustration by Griesbach/Martucci.
Cover design by George Long.
Interior text design by Laura K. Corless.

ISBN: 978-0-425-25141-6

BERKLEY® PRIME CRIME
Berkley Prime Crime Books are published by The Berkley Publishing Group,
a division of Penguin Group (USA) Inc.,
375 Hudson Street, New York, New York 10014.
BERKLEY® PRIME CRIME and the PRIME CRIME logo are trademarks of
Penguin Group (USA) Inc.

PRINTED IN THE UNITED STATES OF AMERICA

10 9 8 7 6 5 4 3 2 1

ALWAYS LEARNING   **PEARSON**

To my husband, Bill,
for all that you are, and all that
you allow me to be.

Acknowledgments

Grateful thanks to my editor, Michelle Vega, for your wonderful suggestions and good eye. It's a great pleasure to work with you.

Many thanks to Sam and Alan Willey, for your constant support and help with the research. Your photos and descriptions of the Maine coast are invaluable to me.

Special thanks to my good friend, Mr. Bill, whose watchful eye keeps me on my toes.

1

Clara Quinn was in the act of rearranging a display of cookbooks when she heard the ruckus. It sounded like a big dog in a tizzy. A *really* big dog. After trying for several moments to ignore the commotion, she walked over to the bookstore's window to get a better look.

Outside, the afternoon heat shimmered on the cars passing by, dazzling her eyes. A group of summer visitors wandered along the storefronts, seeking the shade of the striped awnings as they hunted for souvenirs. Some of them paused to watch the cause of the disturbance—a shaggy black and gray dog leaping up and down, barking at a tall, blonde woman.

Clara winced. Roberta Prince, owner of the stationer's next door, would not appreciate being pawed by a dog.

Roberta never appeared in public without perfect makeup, an impeccable hairdo and an immaculate outfit.

One muddy paw print on that slim, white skirt or, worse, the coral silk shirt, and the image would be destroyed. Roberta's day would be ruined, and everyone else around her would feel the repercussions.

As Clara watched, the irate woman backed off into the road. The dog advanced, apparently determined to knock her down. Roberta must have lost her nerve. She turned tail and dashed across to the nearest haven, which just happened to be the Raven's Nest bookstore.

Unfortunately the door was on a strong spring. It didn't close quite fast enough as Roberta charged through it, followed closely by her pursuer.

Roberta yelped and rushed toward the counter. The dog chased after her, its tail thrashing wildly. Colliding with the table, it sent Clara's intricate display of cookbooks tumbling to the floor.

"Hey!" Clara flew over to the animal and grabbed its collar before it could do any more damage. The dog lunged forward, dragging her with it.

"Tatters! *Sit!*"

The loud bellow had come from the open doorway. In all the uproar, Clara hadn't noticed Rick Sanders blocking out the sunlight. Rick owned the hardware store across the street and, by the looks of it, a very unruly animal.

Clara let go of the collar, allowing the big dog to trot around the counter, once more in pursuit of Roberta.

"Get that thing *away* from me!" Roberta flapped her hand at the dog, making it bark once more.

"Tatters!" Rick slammed the door shut behind him and strode forward, one hand raised in the air. "Here, boy. *Now!*"

Tatters ignored him and went on barking—loud, deep barks that seemed to reverberate throughout the shop.

Clara moved around the counter, leaned forward and laid a hand on the back of the dog's neck. "It's all right, Tatters. Just calm down, baby."

Tatters whined and turned his head to look at her.

Cautiously, Roberta moved around the end of the counter. "You need to control that monster," she hissed at Rick as she hurried to the door and hauled it open. "It's a menace."

Rick looked hurt. "He's just a dog. He thought you had more cookies, that's all."

Roberta brushed imaginary hairs from her skirt and sent a disdainful glare at the offending animal. "That's not a dog. It's a . . . big . . . hairy . . . *horse*." With that, she swept out of the shop and disappeared up the street.

Clara met Rick's gaze and burst out laughing. "I guess she's not a dog lover."

Rick's expression was grim. "I can't really blame her. Look at him. He takes up more room than my truck. The thing *is* a menace."

Clara patted the silky coat and received a moist lick on her hand in gratitude. "Oh, he's not yours, then?"

"Not if I can help it." Still scowling, Rick joined her

behind the counter, where Tatters now sat panting, his tongue flopping out of his mouth.

Snapping the leash he held onto the dog's collar, Rick glanced up at her. "You seem to have a way with dogs."

The comment made Clara uncomfortable. She'd spent most of her life hiding the fact that the infamous sixth sense she'd inherited from her family gave her special insights into people's minds. Not only people, it seemed, but animals as well. At least to the point where she could communicate with them in a way they understood. Some of the time, anyway.

The family called it the Quinn Sense. Not everyone inherited it, much to the disgust of Clara's cousin, Stephanie, who owned the Raven's Nest, loved all things paranormal and never got over the fact that the family curse, as Clara called it, had bypassed her.

Born just two months apart and more like sisters than cousins, she and Stephanie had grown up together, planned futures together, dreamed dreams together. They'd eagerly awaited the day when their powers would be fully developed. When they'd realized that Clara had the Quinn Sense and her cousin did not, it had caused an uneasy rift between the two of them. Unspoken, but there all the same.

"Did I say something wrong?"

Clara jumped, realizing that Rick was staring at her, no doubt confused with her silence. "I'm sorry, I was just thinking about Roberta and wondering why Tatters chased her across the street."

Rick made a sound of disgust in his throat. "She came into the store with a handful of cookies for the dog. I don't know how she knew he was there. That woman doesn't miss anything that goes on in Main Street. Or the whole of Finn's Harbor, come to that."

Clare grinned. "She does have an ear for gossip. People are calling her Maine's main mole."

A smile flicked across his face. "Cute. I like it."

"She doesn't."

"Yeah, I can imagine."

"So she gave Tatters the cookies?"

Rick nodded. "I warned her not to, but of course she didn't listen. The dog wasn't happy with what she gave him, so he started sniffing around her, looking for more. She backed off and he took it as a game. Before I could stop him, he'd chased her out of the store and across the street."

Clara couldn't resist another grin. "Yeah, I saw her."

"I had a customer back there thinking about buying a very expensive lawn mower. There's another guy asking where to find City Hall and someone else looking at garden tools. They've probably gone by now. Thanks to this brute."

Clare leaned down to pat the dog's head. "Oh, poor Tatters. You just wanted to play, didn't you?" She looked up at Rick. "Tatters?"

Rick pulled a face at her as he led the dog over to the door. "My ex-wife called him Tatters because he looked a mess when we rescued him from the pound. Lisa fought tooth and nail to keep him after the divorce, and now, all of a sudden, she wants to dump him on me." He hauled open the door, and Tatters made a leap for freedom, dragging Rick hard against the doorjamb.

He grunted with pain, and Clara screwed up her face in sympathy. Rick, it seemed, was not having a good day, what with the disobedient dog and the bandage she'd just noticed adorning the forefinger of his right hand.

Bracing his foot against the wall, Rick hauled on the leash. "She's got a new boyfriend who hates dogs. To be more specific, he hates Tatters. So now I'm supposed to give him a home? What the heck does she think I'm going to do with him? I can't leave him alone in the house. He'll wreck the place the minute I'm gone."

Clara wasn't quite sure how to respond to that. She'd known Rick just a few months, and they'd become friendly enough to talk about a few things on a personal level. This was the first time, however, that Rick had mentioned his ex-wife.

Of course, there were a lot of things she hadn't told him, either, but somehow an ex-wife seemed a very significant part of his past, and the fact he hadn't once spoken of her suggested a pretty bad split between them.

"I'm sure you'll be able to work things out," she said, mostly because Rick was looking at her as if he expected her to solve his problem. "He seems like a sweet dog and just needs a little attention, that's all."

"He needs a lot more than attention. He needs discipline. Look at him. He's just waiting for the chance to break free again." He waved a hand at Tatters, who now stood looking at him, tail wagging, waiting for his master's next move.

Rick's gray eyes were full of desperation when he looked back at her. "I don't suppose you know anyone who could tame this tiger?"

She hesitated, eager to help but unsure what it would entail. She liked Rick. Really liked him. If things had been different, if she'd never met the man of her dreams in New York, only to find out he was a cheat and a liar, she might have encouraged Rick to take their relationship further.

The pain of her breakup, however, was still fresh in her mind. Even though it had been almost a year since she'd moved back to Finn's Harbor, she was far from ready to trust her heart to anyone yet. No one, she'd vowed, was ever going to hurt her that badly again.

As far as Rick was concerned, she'd managed to keep things uncomplicated, and he seemed to be comfortable with that arrangement. She enjoyed his friendship and was careful not to get into situations that could jeopardize that by letting something more personal creep in.

She was still trying to figure out how she could work with the dog without spending too much time with his owner when Rick said quietly, "It's okay. Forget I mentioned it. Maybe I'll just try to find a home for him. Somewhere where he can run about without demolishing everything that he comes in contact with."

He gave her a quick wave before being dragged across the street by the enthusiastic Tatters.

Watching them go, Clara suddenly noticed a tingling awareness washing over her. She knew the sensation well. She was about to hear voices in her head—voices that spoke in riddles and phrases she couldn't understand. Voices that led her down paths she didn't want to go, and put obstacles in her way to prevent her from following her instincts.

Her reaction was automatic and swift. Closing off her mind, she hurried down to the Reading Nook, where a comfortable couch and a pot of coffee awaited her.

Ever since she'd realized that she had the Quinn Sense and Stephanie didn't, she'd felt isolated somehow. Although most of the family had some degree of psychic ability, she'd kept hers a secret. Far from being the empowering, exciting and liberating experience the cousins had imagined, being able to interpret dreams and occasionally read minds and foretell the future had made Clara feel like a freak.

Desperate to regain some sense of normalcy, she'd left Maine to attend college in New York, where no one knew her or her family. She'd soon discovered that, hard as she tried, she couldn't escape the infamous legacy. The Quinn Sense continued to interfere with her life and mess up her mind.

Worse, it was unpredictable—never there when she needed it, and intruding when she least expected it. When the Sense had failed to prevent her from making the biggest mistake of her life, the betrayal was the last straw. On her thirtieth birthday she'd picked up the pieces and come home to Finn's Harbor.

Her cell phone sang out just then, shattering her thoughts. Stephanie's voice buzzed in her ear, full of tension and anxiety as usual.

"Clara! I just read in the *Chronicle* that the sales of e-books are taking over print versions. What are we going to do? I *knew* I shouldn't have leased that store. What was I thinking? This is the absolute *worst* time to own a bookstore!"

Clara sighed. She'd had this conversation with her cousin more than once, and each time Stephanie had been certain she was headed for bankruptcy. "Calm down, Steffie. The world isn't going to end just because a few misinformed fanatics go around waving placards saying it is. Books are going to be around for at least as long as you'll want to sell them."

"Yes, but if everyone is reading them on electronic readers, who's going to buy print books?"

"Everyone who doesn't like electronic readers. More than enough people to keep you in business for a long time, I promise you."

Stephanie's sigh echoed down the line. "I hope you're right. George keeps telling me the same thing, but then husbands always tell their wives what they want to hear. I just can't help feeling I should have opened a knitting shop instead."

Clara rolled her eyes. "You've never knitted anything in your life."

"What difference does that make?"

"You've spent your entire life immersed in magic and

all things paranormal. With all the interest in it now, opening a bookstore specializing in the occult was a brilliant idea, and you are the perfect person to do it, so stop obsessing over things you can't control. The Raven's Nest is doing just fine. Especially since you opened the Reading Nook. Half the town comes here for the coffee and donuts."

"I know you're right." Stephanie paused, then added in a rush, "I just wish I had the Sense, like you. It would have made planning things so much easier."

Deciding this was the perfect time to change the subject, Clara launched into a detailed account of Roberta's confrontation with Rick's dog.

Stephanie laughed through most of it, until Clara mentioned that Rick was thinking of finding the dog a home. "Oh, you can't let him do that!" Now her cousin sounded close to tears. "That poor dog has already lost one home. Think how awful it would be for him to go to strangers. Can't you look after him?"

"Me? Why me? I'm a stranger, too."

"Yes, but you have . . . you know . . ." Stephanie paused, obviously mindful of her cousin's adverse reaction whenever the Quinn Sense was mentioned.

"Just because I get along with dogs doesn't mean I want to adopt one," Clara said firmly. "Besides, can you imagine what my mother would say if I brought a dog that size into the house? She'd have hysterics."

"Well, you keep saying you're tired of living with Aunt Jessie and you want to find an apartment."

"I do, but so far my hunting for one has produced zero opportunities. Besides, an apartment manager is even less likely to view Tatters with a fond eye."

Stephanie giggled. "Tatters. What a ridiculous name."

Clara smiled. "Oddly enough, the name suits him."

"Oh, he sounds adorable. What a shame Rick can't keep him. I feel so bad for him. I wish—" She broke off, raising her voice to yell at an unseen child. "Michael? *Michael!* What are you doing with that tennis racket? *What?* No! You may *not* use it as a sled. Stay away from the stairs. You hear me?"

Clara held the phone away from her ear, well used to her cousin's tirades. Stephanie had three kids, and while Ethan, the eldest, lived in front of his computer and was barely seen or heard, Olivia and Michael spent most of their time seeing who could get into the most trouble.

"Sorry," Stephanie muttered, when apparently peace was restored. "What was I saying? Oh, yes, about the dog. Surely there's some way Rick could keep him? Can't you talk to him? Persuade him to give Tatters a second chance?"

It was time to end the conversation, Clara decided. Her cousin was making her feel guilty, which was ridiculous, of course. She had no good reason to feel guilt over what was Rick's problem and Rick's alone.

After she hung up, she poured herself a cup of coffee and tried to relax, but the uncomfortable feeling still gnawed away at her stomach. She kept seeing the dog's dark brown eyes staring hopefully into hers, his tail slowly swishing back and forth.

There was nothing she could do, she reminded herself. Working full-time in the bookstore and living with her mom were two very good reasons she couldn't devote her time to training a lovable but totally undisciplined dog. Especially one that was almost as tall as her when standing on his hind legs—no mean feat, since she was five feet ten without her shoes.

Nope, Rick would just have to take care of his own problem. She just hoped he'd decide to keep the dog, so she wouldn't have to feel guilty anymore.

That night she dreamed a monster dog was chasing her along the beach. Her feet kept sinking in the sand, and the dog was drawing closer as she fought to outrun him. Then, without warning, he vanished.

She turned and saw him struggling in the ocean, being taken out to sea by massive waves. Horrified, she tried to jump into the water, only to be thrown back by the current. She woke up with a start, her heart beating rapidly, as if she'd actually been running.

Annoyed with herself, she threw the tangled covers aside and leapt out of bed. She was beginning to wish she'd never set eyes on Tatters. It was easy enough to interpret her dream. She was still racked with guilt for what felt like her abandonment of the animal.

She'd thought that her years in New York had toughened her up, but here she was, obsessing over a dog she'd known for all of ten minutes.

It didn't help her mood when her mother stuck a bowl of cereal in front of her covered in fresh raspberries, strawberries and kiwifruit. Jessica Quinn was on a health kick and obviously felt that her daughter should follow her example.

"You don't eat enough fruit and veggies," Jessie said, wagging a finger at her. "How do you expect to stay healthy with a breakfast of toast and coffee?"

Clara gently pushed the plate away. "It hasn't killed me yet."

"You always used to eat a good breakfast, before you went to New York." Jessie sat down to tackle her own bowl of fruit and cereal. "I don't know what happened to you there, but whatever it was, it didn't do you much good."

Clara bit down hard on her toast and nipped the inside of her lip. Eyes watering, she drank down the last of her coffee. She was getting really tired of her mother probing about her past. Ever since Clara's father had died from a heart attack a few years earlier, Jessie had turned to her daughter, taking a vested interest in her life to the point of intrusion.

At first Clara had made allowances, knowing that they were both working through the terrible grief of loss. But as time passed and Jessie's meddling showed no signs of easing up, Clara's tolerance was severely tested.

When she'd made the decision to return to Finn's Harbor, the scarcity of suitable apartments had made living with her mother the only viable option. Promising herself it was only temporary, Clara had put up with Jessie's constant digs and questions, hoping that eventually her mother would grow tired of the inquisition.

She certainly showed no signs of it that morning. "How much longer are you going to work in that bookstore?" she asked as Clara pushed her chair back from the table. "You have a college degree, for heaven's sake. You should be teaching literature, not selling it."

"I've looked for teaching jobs," Clara said, picking up her plate and mug. "You know that. I'd have to move to Portland, and there's no guarantee I'd get one there. Besides, I moved back to Finn's Harbor because I like living here."

"I can't imagine why." Jessie raised a hand to tuck a strand of hair behind her ear. "This is such a dinky little town, it must feel like the back of beyond after living in a city like New York. I mean"—she waved a hand in the air—"what does Finn's Harbor have to offer a woman like you? There are no eligible men to speak of . . . except for perhaps that good-looking charmer who owns the hardware store. Whatever happened to him, anyway? I thought you two were getting cozy."

Clara puffed out her breath. "I have no intention of getting cozy with anyone. I didn't come back here to find a husband, if that's what you think."

Jessie pouted. "I don't know what to think. You've never told anyone why you left a glamorous, exciting life in one of the most stimulating cities in the world to hibernate in a town that's invaded by strangers in the summer and pulls up the sidewalks in the winter."

Carrying her plate and mug, Clara headed for the

kitchen. "I told you, I missed living here. I'm happy here, and that's all that matters."

"Are you?" Jessie followed her into the kitchen. "You don't seem all that happy to me. You've changed, Clara, and I wish I knew why."

Clara put her plate and mug in the dishwasher and turned to her mother. "I'm fine, Mom. You worry about me far too much. Why don't you start living your own life again, instead of trying to live mine? You have friends. You could travel. Go on vacation somewhere."

Jessie sighed. "I'd rather go with you."

"I don't have time. I'm busy helping Steffie at the store." Clara leaned forward and planted a kiss on her mother's cheek. "Quit worrying about me. I'm fine."

"That's what your father said the day he had his heart attack."

Clara rolled her eyes. "It is not the same thing and you know it. Now I have to go, or I'll be late for work. I've got a ton of errands to run before I can go to the bookstore." She rushed out the door before her mother could think of something else to say to upset her. Something told her this was not going to be her day.

The feeling persisted all morning, growing even stronger as she finally drove to Main Street and parked the car halfway up the steep hill. Climbing out, she pulled in a deep breath. Clapboard storefronts lined the hillside street in a parade of pastel pink, blue and yellow. Below them, boats of all shapes and sizes crowded the harbor, while farther out white sails dipped and swayed across the deep blue water.

Pausing for a moment, Clara watched the seagulls floating above the sands against the hazy smudge of mountains that guarded the bay. Before she'd left for college she'd taken the scenery for granted. Once in New York, however, she'd missed the ocean and the peaceful ambiance of her hometown. Now that she'd learned to appreciate the beauty of Finn's Harbor, she took the time to drink in the view.

Usually the fresh sea air helped to clear her mind, but today it failed to revive her. It was almost noon, and already the sticky heat of the day seemed overpowering. The climb to the top of the hill didn't help, and by the time she reached the bookstore she was sweltering, out of breath and longing for a glass of iced tea.

The feeling of anxiety that had bothered her ever since she'd fallen out of bed that morning was now a full-blown feeling of impending disaster. Hoping it wasn't the Quinn Sense giving her a warning, she shoved open the door and stepped inside the cool, shadowed entrance of the Raven's Nest.

When Stephanie had first asked her cousin to take the afternoon shift at the bookstore, Clara had agreed with the clear understanding it was only temporary—just until Stephanie found someone else to help out.

Clara had returned home from New York with the firm intention of finding an apartment and a job. In a town as small as Finn's Harbor, however, teaching positions were few and far between. The commute to Portland, the closest big city, was too long to be an option, and the one offer she'd been given closer to home had not appealed to her.

Stephanie seemed in no hurry to replace her, and after working at the bookstore for several months, Clara had settled into a relaxing, if slightly mundane routine. She was in a comfortable place right now and didn't seem to have the incentive to look for another job.

Although she tended to avoid anything to do with magic and the occult, the bookstore had grown on her. The dangling beads and spinning crystals, the lifesize fortune-teller staring into her crystal ball and the stuffed raven keeping watch from its high perch appealed to the quirky side of her nature. Besides, Stephanie needed her, and it felt good to be helping her cousin make a success of the Raven's Nest.

As Clara walked over to the counter, Stephanie called out to her. Balanced on the rung of a ladder and half-hidden behind a stack of books, she peered out from one of the aisles. "Have you heard the news?"

Clara paused. The sensation was back. She could hear them now—the voices, clamoring in her head. She struggled to banish them. "What news?"

A face popped up from behind the counter, crowned with flyaway red hair. Molly Owens's bright blue eyes sparkled with excitement. "We've been waiting for you to get here. You won't believe what's happened. There's been a murder!"

The voices were immediately silenced, leaving only a

cold sick feeling behind. Clara's lips felt dry as she answered Molly. "Where? Here in Finn's Harbor?"

Stephanie abandoned her books and hurried over to join her young assistant behind the counter. "We thought you might have heard it on the news."

Clara shook her head. "I was listening to a CD in my car. Who died? Not anyone we know, I hope."

Molly was practically jumping up and down. "No one knows who he is. The police found him this morning. Guess where!"

You don't want to know. Clara jumped. It was as if someone had spoken the words out loud in her ear. She looked at Stephanie for help.

Her cousin's face was a picture of discomfort. "I'm sorry, Clara. I know you like him, but . . ." She hesitated, and before Clara could absorb the words, Molly jumped in to finish for her.

"They found the body in the back of Rick Sanders's truck!"

2

Clara kept staring at her cousin, waiting desperately for her to say that Molly was joking. Instead, Stephanie slowly nodded her head. "It's true. Roberta was in here a little while ago. She heard it from John Halloran. He's taking care of the store until Rick gets back."

Clara clutched the edge of the counter. "What happened?"

Molly started to say something, but Stephanie cut her off. "Molly, go make a fresh pot of coffee, would you?"

The young girl looked disappointed, but she wandered off to the Reading Nook, leaving the cousins alone.

"We don't know much," Stephanie said, opening the cash drawer and closing it again. "Just that the body was found in Rick's truck and he's down at the station helping the police in their inquiries."

"Well, they can't possibly think he killed someone." Clara hurried behind the counter and stashed her purse on the shelf underneath. "Dan must know that."

Stephanie shrugged. "Dan Petersen's the chief of police. I guess he has to question everyone."

"Yeah, I remember when he questioned Molly about Ana Jordan's death. He was convinced Molly had killed her."

"Well, that turned out all right in the end, though, didn't it?" Stephanie patted her arm. "Don't worry, Clara. If Rick is innocent, I'm sure Dan will know it. He's a good cop."

Clara turned on her. "*If?* There's no *if* about it. Rick would never kill anyone."

Stephanie held up her hands. "Okay! If that's so, then he has nothing to worry about."

Annoyed with herself for overreacting, Clara shrugged. "So who's the victim, anyway?"

"They don't know his name yet. John said he thought the guy was from out of town."

"A tourist?"

"I guess so." Stephanie looked worried. "Clara, you're not going to get involved in this, are you? Remember what happened the last time. You almost got yourself killed."

"Of course I'm not getting involved. Besides, if I remember correctly, you were the one who begged me to look into Ana's murder."

"That's because everyone thought Molly had killed her. Rick Sanders can take care of himself."

Clara glanced at the clock. "Isn't it time you left to pick up your kids? Aunt Paula will be wondering where you are."

Stephanie followed her gaze and ran a hand through her fair hair. "Oh crap. Mom will kill me. She's got a dentist appointment this afternoon." She snatched up a large tapestry purse and tucked it under her arm. "I'll let you know if I hear anything else."

"Do that."

Stephanie paused at the door and looked back. "You will talk to me before you do anything . . . rash, won't you?"

"I'm not going to do anything rash. Besides, I'm sure Rick will be back in the store this afternoon, so you have nothing to worry about."

Stephanie looked unconvinced. "I hope so. Let me know if you hear anything." The door closed behind her, and Clara slumped against the counter, wishing she felt as positive as she'd sounded.

Shreds of her dream kept wafting through her mind. What was happening to Tatters while Rick was detained? Was the dog alone in the house, tearing it apart? Was he in the hardware store, creating havoc?

Fortunately, she didn't have time to worry about it as a little rush of customers took her mind off things.

Shortly before Molly was due to leave, Clara caught sight of Rick entering his store across the street. She waited until Molly had finished serving her customer, and hurried over to her.

"I'm going to the hardware store to see if everything's all right over there," she said as Molly finished entering the purchase on the computer. "Rick's back, so at least he wasn't arrested."

Molly gave her a grin. "All right! Go ahead, I'll wait."

"I won't be long." Clara was out of the door before the words had left her mouth.

The sun scorched her head as she waited on the curb for the line of slow-moving cars to pass. Losing patience, she darted in between a pickup pulling a fifth wheel, and a black SUV piloted by a white-haired man who gestured at her as she flashed by him.

Rick had his back to her when she rushed into the shop. He stood talking to John Halloran, his sometimes assistant, who kept nodding his head and looking sympathetic.

Clara wasn't sure how she felt about John. He'd owned a candy store farther down the street when she and Stephanie were kids. They'd been convinced he was an evil wizard. There was something in the way he'd talked to them that had freaked them out, and even now Clara felt uneasy whenever he was around.

John saw her coming and gave her a brief nod of his head.

Rick turned around, his taut features breaking into a smile at the sight of her.

"I heard the news," Clara blurted out before he could say anything. "I'm so sorry, Rick. Is there anything I can do? I mean . . . I hope . . ." She let her voice trail off, not sure quite what to say.

"It's okay," Rick assured her. "I wasn't arrested or anything."

He was still smiling, but she could see the worry in his eyes. "What did Dan say? Do they know who did it?"

"Nope." Rick looked back at John. "You can run along now, buddy. I can take it from here."

"You sure?" John gave Clara a long look that somehow made her feel she was intruding, then ambled out the door and disappeared.

Rick gazed after him, a frown creasing his brow. "I've got to get a permanent assistant. John's been good about helping out now and then, but I need someone here to take over full-time when I'm away."

Clara looked at him in alarm. "Are you saying you're expecting to be arrested?"

He turned away before she could see his expression. "No, of course not. Still, you never know what might happen. If I'm sick, for instance, or have to go out of town for something, I have to rely on John being free to take over. With a permanent assistant I wouldn't have that worry."

"True." Clara ran her fingers along the edge of the counter. "So, did Dan tell you anything about the murder?"

He looked at her then, his head tilted to one side. "You're not thinking of hunting down a killer again, are you?"

Clara laughed. "Not on your life. I had all the excitement I needed with the last one."

He looked relieved. "Good. Messing with police business is dangerous stuff."

She wondered for a moment if he was warning her off for a reason, then dismissed it. "I heard that the cops don't know the victim's identity."

"You heard right." Rick walked over to the shelves and straightened up some boxes of patio lights.

Clara followed him. "He must be from out of town."

Rick dropped his hand and turned to face her. "You're not going to quit until I tell you everything. Right?"

She grinned. "Right."

"Okay. Apparently a truck driver going past my house early this morning spotted the body in the back of my pickup and called the cops. Dan asked me a lot of questions about where I was and what I was doing last night. I told him I was at the bowling alley until around ten or so, then left and went home. I have no idea how or when the body landed in my truck. Dan said he'd been killed with a blunt instrument. So far they haven't found the murder weapon, but they're searching the area around the bowling alley."

Clara could tell now that although Rick was putting on a brave face, underneath he was worried. As well he might be. "We'd better hope they don't find it there," she murmured.

"Exactly." Rick strode over to the counter and opened up a box of miniature flashlights. "Things look bad enough for me right now, but if they find the murder weapon anywhere near that bowling alley, I'll be calling my lawyer."

Clara was about to answer him when she was interrupted by whining, accompanied by scratching, from the door that led into the rear of the shop. "You've still got Tatters!"

"As if I don't have enough problems." Rick glanced at the door. "I still can't make up my mind what to do with him. I could take him to the pound in Portland, I guess—"

"No!" Clara's cry of distress cut off his words. "You can't do that! He could be put down."

As if to echo her words, the whining and scratching intensified.

Rick lifted his shoulders in a resigned shrug. "What else can I do? He's not happy locked up back there, and he's even more miserable shut up in the garage at home. I don't know what else to do."

Clara drew a deep breath. "What if I helped take care of him?"

She regretted the words the moment they were out of her mouth, but it was too late now. Rick was looking at her as if she had thrown him a life preserver. "That would be great! What do you have in mind?"

"I don't know. I haven't thought it through yet. I just . . ." She threw a glance at the door, which was still bearing the brunt of Tatters' claws. "I can't bear the thought of him going to the pound."

"Look, you don't have to do anything." Rick gestured

at the door. "He can be a handful, and you have to work and probably don't have time to deal with him. If you feel that bad about it I won't take him to the pound. I'll try to find him a home somewhere."

Now that she'd embraced the idea, she was reluctant to let it go. "I'll work out something, I promise." She started for the door. "Give me some time to think about it."

"Why don't we talk about it over dinner? Do you like Italian food? Angelo's is pretty decent, and they make a great tiramisu." He was following her out the door, seemingly intent on getting an answer from her.

She paused on the street to look back at him. When she'd first started working at the Raven's Nest, he'd invited her out more than once. She'd turned him down so often he'd finally given up asking her. She'd never quite decided if she was sad or sorry about that.

Now he was asking her again, but this time it seemed less threatening, more of a business meeting than an actual date. She saw his expression change, as if he had already accepted her refusal. Before he could speak, she blurted out, "I love tiramisu. It's my favorite dessert. When did you want to go?"

The surprised pleasure on his face warmed her. "No time like the present. Tonight?"

She hesitated. "Tomorrow's my day off. Can we make it then?"

"Sure. Want me to pick you up?"

Clara had a vision of her mother hovering over him at the door. "Why don't I meet you there?"

"Fine. Eight thirty?"

She smiled. "I'll be there."

Something in his eyes made her nervous. With a quick wave she spun around, intent on dashing across the road to the bookstore. Instead, she almost ran into Roberta Prince.

The woman stood right in front of her, blocking her way. "I was wondering when you were going to give someone else a chance to get through the door," she snapped, her eyes blazing with hostility.

"Sorry," Clara muttered, and darted around her to cross the road. Reaching the door of the Raven's Nest, she glanced back, just in time to see Roberta disappearing into the hardware store.

"Good timing," Molly said from behind the counter. "I was just getting ready to leave."

"Sorry," Clara said again, letting the door close behind her. "I was talking to Rick about the murder."

Molly halted her rush to the door. "What'd he say? Do they know who did it? Who the victim is? Do they think Rick did it?"

Clara leaned her back against the counter. "No, no and especially no. They're still looking for the murder weapon."

Molly gave an exaggerated shiver. "It's hard to believe we have another murder in Finn's Harbor. At least this one wasn't in our store."

"Neither is it anyone we know." Clara moved behind the counter. "I guess that's some reason to be thankful."

"Yeah, but there's still a murderer running around out there." Molly paused again on the doorstep. "I'm locking my windows tonight." She wagged a finger at Clara. "Just be careful when you walk down the hill to your car. You never know who could be lurking about, looking for another victim."

"Personally, I think it's all kind of exciting."

The soft voice had spoken from behind her, and Molly spun around so fast she almost lost her balance.

John Halloran appeared at her side, his teeth bared in a grin. "Going somewhere?"

Molly gave him her best scowl and disappeared into the street.

Bracing herself, Clara greeted her customer. "What can I do for you?"

John sidled up to the counter, looking over his shoulder as if checking to see if they were alone. "A little bird told me you had a new Wayne Lester book in."

"We do, though they're not out on the shelves yet. If you want to wait a minute, I'll go and get you a copy." She moved to the end of the counter, then stopped as John edged up alongside her.

"So, what do you think about this murder business then?" His dark eyes gleamed at her through the lenses of his black-rimmed glasses.

She backed off a little. John's attempts to comb his gray hair over his bald patch left it in little spikes along his forehead. He looked a little like an aging clown. Clara was not fond of clowns. "I hope they catch whoever did it and put him in jail."

"Strange that the body ended up in Rick's truck, don't you think?"

Clara stiffened. She couldn't imagine why Rick would hire John Halloran to work in his store. The man seemed to get a perverse delight out of other people's troubles. "I guess the killer had to hide the body somewhere. It must be horrible for Rick."

"Even worse for the guy in the back of the truck." John chuckled at his own ghoulish joke.

"I'll get that book for you." Clara rushed past him and down to the stockroom. It took her a while to find the book, and by the time she carried it back to the counter, John was talking to another customer.

Clara wasn't really surprised to hear the two of them discussing the murder with disgusting relish. Mrs. Riley was a notorious gossip. She and Roberta Prince made a fine pair.

The elderly woman was hanging on to John's words as if he were reading a long-awaited will.

"Can't say I'm all that surprised," John was saying. "Rick's a bit of a mystery. Doesn't talk much about his personal life. I always say quiet guys like that have something to hide."

"I heard he used to be married," Mrs. Riley murmured. "Wonder what happened to his wife."

"She's alive and well," Clara said sharply. She darted behind the counter and rang up the purchase, then waited for John to swipe his card.

"Do you know her then?" Mrs. Riley's sharp eyes probed Clara's face.

"I know she just gave Rick a dog." Clara bagged the book and handed it over to John with his receipt.

He took it with a smirk. "Guess you know him better than any of us."

Clara scowled. "What exactly does that mean?"

"Nothing!" John sauntered over to the door. "Nothing at all. But if I were you, I'd be careful who I trust around here."

He was out of the door before she could answer.

Mrs. Riley sniffed. "You never know who you're dealing with these days, that's what I say." She trotted off down the aisles, leaving Clara fuming behind the counter. Everyone was so quick to judge. The same thing that had happened to Molly was happening now to Rick. She hoped fervently that Dan would find out who killed that poor man and put an end to all the speculation before some real damage was done.

She was still seething about the injustice of it all when she arrived home that evening. Jessie had fixed a shrimp salad for her, and she ate it in the kitchen, while her mother poured a couple of glasses of wine.

"I saw on the news that your friend at the hardware store is in trouble," she said as she sat down opposite Clara at the kitchen table.

Clara swallowed a mouthful of lettuce before answering her. "He's not in trouble. Someone dumped a dead body in his truck, that's all."

Jessie raised her perfectly plucked eyebrows. "You don't find that unusual?"

Clara regarded her mother with a jaundiced eye. For the past year Jessie had been striving to regain some of her youthful looks. She'd had her hair cut and dyed in a short, flip-up style with highlights. She spent numerous hours at the gym and bought her clothes with a keen eye for fashion. Tonight she wore a red, low-cut top and white pants that clung to her hips. It was obvious to Clara that her mother was phasing out the mourning period and was ready to move on with her life. The thought both pleased and worried her. Jessie was apt to be impulsive at times, and not always discreet. In a town the size of Finn's Harbor, very little escaped the grapevine.

"I think," Clara said slowly, "that Rick's truck was in the wrong place at the wrong time. If he'd killed that man, why on earth would he leave the body out in the open for everyone to see? "

"Perhaps he was waiting for the right moment to get rid of it." She paused. "You know that they think they've found the murder weapon, I suppose."

Clara almost choked on her dinner roll. "No, I didn't know that."

"It was found in the bushes alongside the parking lot between the bowling alley and the driving range."

The voices. They were echoing in her head. Whispering, as they always did, insistent and disturbing. She shut them off before she could make sense of the words. "I have to call Stephanie." She glanced at the clock as she pushed her chair back. "She'll be wondering where I am."

Her cousin must have been waiting for her nightly call, as she answered on the first ring. "Clara? Did you see the news? It's all over the TV."

"I haven't seen it yet." Clara's fingers tightened on her cell. "Mom told me they'd found the murder weapon."

"The police *think* it's the murder weapon. It was found in the parking lot of the bowling alley."

"So I heard."

"It looks as if the dead guy was killed there."

"Probably."

"While Rick was there."

Clara briefly closed her eyes. "Just because the body ended up in his truck doesn't mean he killed the guy. Whoever killed him must have dumped the body in there to get rid of it."

"Funny that Rick didn't see it when he drove home."

"He probably didn't look in the back. It was dark when he went home."

"You know everyone is going to think he did it, don't you?"

"More than likely. I have faith in Dan and his guys, though. They'll find the real murderer."

"They don't even know the name of the victim. They had Rick down at the station again tonight to see if he knew the guy. Deanne Summers interviewed him on the way out. Rick said he'd never seen the guy before."

The voices again. Only one this time. She tried to

ignore it, but the words sounded clearly in her ear. *He's lying.*

Rattled, she spoke out loud. "What the heck does that mean?"

Stephanie's startled voice banished the whispering. "I think it means he didn't know . . . oh, wait a minute." Her voice faded as she moved away from the phone. "Olivia! How many times do I have to tell you not to put Jasper in the laundry basket. No, he doesn't like it. That's why he claws his way out of there. Olivia! Take him out. *Now!*" There was a pause before she spoke again. "I've got to go. The cat's got his claws stuck in a sweater. Is everything okay in the shop?"

"Everything's fine. Hope your sweater's okay."

"So do I." Again Stephanie paused, then added in a rush, "Clara, if Rick is in trouble, be careful, okay?"

"I'm always careful. Go rescue your sweater." Clara closed her cell, her forehead creased in a frown. She did her best to ignore the voices, but every once in a while there was nothing she could do to shut them out. The Quinn Sense was unpredictable and spasmodic at best. Yet it was never wrong. It might not always be there when she needed it, but when the voices spoke, they spoke the truth.

It was a relief when her mother announced she was going to bed early to read. Jessie worked at the local library and was never short of reading material. Clara wished her good-night, then settled down in front of the TV to watch one of her favorite cop shows. She found it hard to concentrate, however, and instead her mind kept wandering back to her conversation with Rick that afternoon.

She could hear him now, his voice tense with concern. *If they find the murder weapon anywhere near that bowling alley, I'll be calling my lawyer.* Had he called his lawyer? she wondered. Had it gone that far? If so, the gossips' tongues would be wagging overtime.

Poor Rick. What would happen to Tatters if his master got arrested? In the next instant she chided herself. Of course Rick wouldn't be arrested. He'd done nothing wrong. Yet again she heard his voice. *I need someone here to take over full-time when I'm away.* It was as if he expected to be gone for a length of time.

With a start she realized that her show had ended and the news was on. The top story of the night was, of course, the murder. There was a picture of the bowling alley and a rerun of Rick's interview with Deanne Summers.

It was obvious the news reporter had ambitions. She kept waving the microphone in Rick's face, demanding he answer her questions. The few words he did say came out more from frustration than anything.

The scene switched back to the studio, where Tom Wright, the news anchor, was commenting on the interview. "Breaking news," he said, sounding as if he couldn't wait to wrap up the broadcast and go home. "The murder weapon found in the vicinity of the Harbor Bowling Alley has been identified. It's a specialty hammer, apparently obtained from Parson's Hardware Store. Police also found spatters of blood that confirm the victim was killed in the parking lot of the bowling alley. The owner of the hardware store, Rick Sanders, also owns the truck in which the body was found. The police have been questioning him—"

The voices spoke, loud and clear. *Suspect number one.*

3

Determined not to listen to the annoying whispers in her ear, Clara grabbed the remote and turned up the volume. Tom had introduced Carson Dexter, the mayor of Finn's Harbor. Carson looked as if he'd just fallen out of bed. His light brown hair, usually combed neatly back from his forehead, flopped over his eyebrows, and he kept rubbing his chin as if he needed a shave.

"This is utterly disgraceful," he exclaimed, his eyes wide and staring at the camera. "A murder here in our little town of Finn's Harbor is totally unacceptable. I have demanded that the police department make every effort to hunt down the perpetrator of this vicious crime and bring down on him the full power of the justice system. I urge each and every one of you to come forward with any information that might be helpful in this case, no matter how trivial it might seem. Together we will find this brutal killer, so that the citizens of this town may once more sleep peacefully in their beds."

He's afraid, Clara thought. No doubt worried about his two young daughters. She'd seen pictures of the girls, both preteens, and both resembling their mother with their long, silky-straight blonde hair and expensive clothes. It must be difficult being a father while in the public eye. The chance of his children being a target for a disgruntled constituent had to be forever in his mind—one of the drawbacks of being a politician.

She turned off the TV, her mind drawn back to Rick as she got ready for bed. Things looked bad for him. She couldn't seem to silence the voice that kept repeating in her ear. *He's lying.* She didn't want to believe that. Why would Rick lie if he had nothing to hide?

She slept badly that night and awoke to hear her mother tapping on her bedroom door.

"I'm just leaving," her mother called out when Clara answered her knock. "You might want to read the *Chronicle* before you leave. It's full of news about the murder."

Clara rolled onto her back and stared at the ceiling until she heard the front door snap shut. Ten minutes later she was still wide awake and burning to see what was in the newspaper.

She made herself wait until she was showered and dressed before settling down at the kitchen table with a cup of coffee. Picking up the paper, the first thing she saw was a picture of the murdered man on the front page.

Underneath, the caption explained that although the police were reluctant to print a picture of a dead man, all attempts to identify him had failed and they felt that publishing the photo might help them in their investigation.

Clara was grateful to note that whoever had taken the picture had taken care to disguise the head wounds that had killed the victim. She studied the photo but could see nothing familiar about the face. He appeared to be a fairly young man, about her own age, with fair hair and a scruffy chin. Clara hoped that his relatives would learn of his death before seeing it splashed all over the front page of a newspaper. How sad for his parents. Had he left behind a wife and children? She hoped not.

The article also mentioned that Rick's truck was involved and that the murder weapon had come from his store. The reporter had been careful not to suggest that Rick was responsible for the murder, but the insinuation was there.

Feeling depressed, Clara washed down a slice of toast with the rest of the coffee. It was Wednesday, her day off, and she had nothing to do except perhaps go on another fruitless hunt for an apartment. Idly she turned the rest of the pages and saw an ad for a farmer's market on the seafront. She was still trying to decide whether to brave the heat and visit the market or spend the day in air-conditioning when her cell phone sang its tune.

"Clara! Have you seen the newspaper?" Stephanie was almost choking with excitement. "It has a picture of the victim in there."

"I saw it." The last thing she wanted right then was to discuss the murder.

Stephanie, however, seemed determined to talk about it. "Did you recognize him? George said he looked familiar but wasn't sure. I don't think I've ever seen him around here. He must be a tourist, don't you think? Did you hear that the murder weapon came from Rick's store? "

"Yes, I did." Clara took a deep breath. "I'm sorry, Steffie. I'm just on my way out. I'll call you later, okay?"

Stephanie sounded disappointed as she said good-bye, and Clara felt guilty for cutting their chat short. She just wasn't in the mood for conversation and decided the best thing she could do was take herself off to the market and get some fresh air to clear her mind. Since she and her cousin had agreed to take only one day off a week, she might as well make the most of it.

Arriving there a few minutes later, she instantly regretted her impulse. There were so many people milling around it was close to impossible to get near any of the stalls. After jostling for space in front of a fruit stand, Clara bought a bag of cherries, then fought her way through the crowd to the seafront.

Sitting on the seawall facing the ocean, she popped a cherry in her mouth. The water shimmered in the sun, making her blink in spite of her sunglasses. On the distant horizon she could see a fuzzy line of gray. Possibly a storm brewing.

The cherry was sweet and juicy, and she reached for another. Just at that moment a familiar voice called out her name. Inwardly groaning, Clara spat out the pit and dropped it in the bag before greeting the woman standing behind her.

As always, Roberta Prince stood out in the crowd. Wearing an orange silk shirt and short beige skirt, her sleek blonde hair tucked into a wide-brimmed hat, Roberta could easily have passed for a famous movie star. More than one bored husband slid a sly glance her way as he passed, and although Roberta gave no sign she'd noticed, Clara knew she was eating up all the attention.

"How come you're not at the bookstore?" For a moment it seemed that Roberta would sit down next to her, but then she paused and looked in disgust at the grubby wall.

"Day off," Clara said briefly.

"Ah!" Roberta stared out across the bay, where a man on skis swooped back and forth behind a speeding boat. "I hear that Rick may be in trouble with the police."

Clara fought down her irritation. "Oh? Where did you hear that?"

Roberta looked at her as if she had lost her mind. "How could you not know? It's all over the TV and the newspapers. He's suspected of murdering that poor man."

"He's not a suspect, as far as I know." Clara ignored the whispering in her ear. "He's just helping the police in their investigation, that's all."

Roberta rolled her eyes. "Clara, dear. Everyone knows that's police jargon for suspecting him of murder."

"They haven't arrested him."

"Only a matter of time."

Clara glared at her. "You know as well as I do that Rick would never hurt anyone, much less kill someone."

Considering that the woman was supposed to be madly in love with him, she wasn't displaying much loyalty as to his innocence. Roberta had made no secret of the fact that she had pegged Rick Sanders to be her third husband. The fact that Rick was strongly resisting all her efforts to convince him of that hadn't deterred her at all. She never missed an opportunity to remind Clara that he was off-limits, despite the fact that Clara had never given her any indication that she was interested in him.

"Of course I know that." The wind caught the brim of Roberta's hat, and she lifted a hand to straighten it. "The police, however, don't know him as well as I do. Carson Dexter is demanding they arrest someone for the murder, and he's putting pressure on Dan. Rick is the only suspect he has, and it's only a matter of time before he arrests him to keep the mayor off his back."

There was a grain of truth in what she said, and that worried Clara. She wasn't about to give Roberta that satisfaction, however. Besides, neither one of them knew the whole story. She would see Rick that evening. Maybe she'd know more then. It occurred to her that Roberta would not be happy to hear Clara was having dinner with her intended.

For a moment Clara was tempted to tell her, then decided she had enough on her mind without antagonizing the woman. She got up from the wall and brushed the back of her shorts. "Well, I'm sure everything will get sorted out once the police identify the victim."

"Maybe. But I have a feeling that things are going to get messy for Rick before this is over."

Clara answered that with a farewell wave and headed off to her car. The words stayed with her, however, and it didn't help that they were echoed by the voices of the Quinn Sense whispering in her ear.

She spent the rest of the day driving to the outlet mall in nearby Mittleford to find something to wear for her meeting with Rick that night. She refused to think of it as a date. It was safer that way.

After browsing through the racks of the fashion outlets, she finally decided on a sleeveless ruffled top in tropical blue to go with her white pants, and just because she liked it, a bright yellow sundress. Happy with her purchases, she drove home, trying not to think about the cloud hanging over Rick's head. Maybe tonight, for a little while at least, she could take his mind off his troubles.

Jessie, as usual, hovered near the front door as Clara prepared to leave that night. "You look nice," she said, viewing the blue top with a critical eye. "That color goes well with your dark hair and eyes. You certainly don't take after your father's side of the family. The Quinns are all like Stephanie—fair-haired and blue-eyed. It must be their Irish inheritance. We can thank the Irish side of the family for the Quinn Sense. Your father told me it was a gift from the leprechauns."

Clara stared at her mother. It wasn't the first time she'd heard the supposed origin of the Sense, by any means. It was, however, the first time her mother had mentioned

her father in almost a year. It was also the first time she
had mentioned the Quinn Sense since before Clara had
left for New York eleven years ago.

Why now? She was on the verge of asking her mother
that question, when good sense prevailed. This wasn't the
time for a discussion on the subject. Even Jessie didn't
know that her daughter had inherited the strange powers,
and Clara was determined to keep it that way.

She murmured, "Thank you," instead, and opened the
front door.

She had almost escaped through it when Jessie called
out, "You didn't tell me where you're going."

Clara sighed. She'd hoped to avoid the inevitable inquisition that would follow when her mother learned about
her meeting with Rick. At least she could postpone it for
the time being. "I'm meeting a friend for dinner," she
said, closing the door. "I won't be late."

Climbing into her car, she felt guilty for leaving her
mother in the dark. Jessie would probably pout all evening
until her daughter came home and filled in all the details.
Until then, Clara told herself, she would put everything
out of her mind and concentrate on the evening ahead.

The sun had begun its descent behind the mountains
as she drove along the coast road to the restaurant. Angelo's sat on the very brink of the bay, hovering above the
ocean at the edge of the cliffs. It afforded a great view of
the ocean on one side, and the red roofs and white walls
of Finn's Harbor on the other.

By the time she'd parked and had been escorted to a

table by the window, however, the sun had set and all she could see was a faint outline of the mountains and the twinkling lights of the town reflected on the water.

Rick had not yet arrived, and she fidgeted with her wineglass, trying to ignore the fluttering feeling in the region of her stomach. She had no reason to be nervous, she told herself. This wasn't a date. Not a real date. Besides, it wasn't as if she didn't know Rick.

Do you really know him? Clara started, unprepared for the whispering in her ear. Was that the Sense, or her own instincts kicking in?

She'd asked herself that same question so often it was automatic. There had been a time when she had trusted her instincts and relied on them far more than her infamous inheritance. Until she'd met the man she'd wanted to marry, until he'd betrayed her in the worst way. Neither her instincts nor the Sense had saved her from the pain and humiliation of that relationship. Now she no longer trusted either of them and strove with all her might to ignore the voices that intruded and tormented her.

"You're looking really fierce," a deep voice said above her head. "Am I that late?"

She glanced up to see Rick looking down at her. He was smiling, but she could see the uncertainty in his expression and was immediately apologetic. She'd turned him down so many times it was no wonder he was uneasy.

"No, of course not." She smiled up at him. "I was thinking about . . ." She was going to say the murder, but under the circumstances, that didn't seem a good way to open the conversation. "My mother," she said after a short pause.

Rick didn't look too convinced as he took a seat opposite her. "Sorry I kept you waiting." He glanced at his watch. "Tatters decided to make a run for it as I was coming out the door. I had to chase him around four blocks before I finally got hold of him."

Clara hid a grin. "Have you been taking him for walks?"

Rick raised an eyebrow. "Walks? That dog doesn't know the meaning of the word. His idea of a walk is to lunge at everything that moves, and if it looks like it's getting away from him, he takes off after it, dragging me with him."

She studied him for a moment before answering. He didn't look like a man accused of murder. In fact, now that he'd been reassured she wasn't going to jump up and run away, he seemed perfectly relaxed and ready to enjoy the evening. "How are you doing?" she asked, trying not to sound as if doomsday were just around the corner.

"I'm doing fine. How are you doing?"

"You know what I mean."

The humor faded from his gray eyes. "I think I could be in a lot of trouble."

"I'm sorry." She had an insane urge to reach across the table and grasp his hand. Resisting it with some difficulty, she added, "They still haven't identified the victim?"

"As far as I know." He glanced around the room, as if

to make sure no one could hear him. "They found the murder weapon. It came from my store, and it was found just a few yards away from where my truck was parked."

"Yes, I know. I saw it in the paper."

"Unfortunately the killer had gone to the trouble of wiping it clean, so no prints. Dan wanted me to take a look at the body. I told him I'd never seen the guy before. I also told him I think someone is trying to frame me."

Shocked, she stared at him. "Who would want to do that?"

"I have no idea. I don't have any enemies. At least, I thought I didn't." He leaned forward and lowered his voice. "Why else would someone use a tool from my store to kill someone and dump the dead body in my truck?"

"I can't imagine. I—" She paused as the whispers interrupted her thoughts. *They're not related.* Not sure what that meant, she struggled to finish what she was going to say. "I . . . they may not be related."

She hadn't meant to repeat what the voice had told her. Rick was looking at her as if she'd said something radical. "What does that mean?"

She wished she knew. Groping blindly for an explanation, she said slowly, "Well, think about it. Parson's Hardware is the only place in town that sells specialty hammers, so it's not surprising the murder weapon came from your store." She frowned. "How did the police know that's where it came from?"

"It still had the price tag attached to it."

"Oh, so it wasn't something that had been used a lot, then."

"Exactly. When I checked the inventory, there was one missing. Whoever took it didn't bother to pay for it. I think it was taken specifically for the purpose of committing murder."

Clara shivered. "Even if it was, how would the killer know you would be at the bowling alley that night? Did you tell anyone you were going there?"

"Only Tatters, and I don't think he would pass it on to anyone."

She wrinkled her nose at him. "Funny. Well, *I* think your truck just happened to be in the parking lot at the time of the murder and provided the perfect hiding place to get rid of the body."

Rick gave her a look that almost made her forget she was supposed to be off men. "Thank you. You might be the only one in town who thinks that."

"Of course I'm not. Anyone who knows you would know you're no killer."

"Look around."

Startled, she did as he asked. Glancing at the other tables, she noticed several of the other diners quickly turning their heads. "Let them look," she muttered. "What do they know?"

"Only what they read in the paper and hear on TV."

She shook her head. "Is there anything I can do to help?"

His smile was lopsided this time. "Yeah. Find out who killed the guy."

She knew he was joking. He didn't really mean for her to track down a murderer. She wasn't surprised when the voices started whispering in her head. To get rid of them she said loudly, "I wish I could."

"So do I." He looked up as the server approached. "Let's not talk about this anymore, okay?"

She was happy to drop the subject, and concentrated on the menu instead. After deliberating for a while, she finally decided on the ravioli, and agreed with enthusiasm when Rick suggested a bottle of Chianti.

"So tell me," Rick said, as he handed her the bread plate, "what did you do with your day off?"

She took a slice of bread and reached for the olive oil. "I went to the market. I ran into Roberta there."

Rick uttered a soft groan. "Don't tell me. She's already got me locked up in jail for murder, right?"

Clara grinned. "She's very concerned about you."

"That's even worse. She'll be hovering over me like a mother duck."

"You know you enjoy that."

"Yeah, like I enjoy a root canal."

"She means well."

Rick rolled his eyes. "They said that about Mussolini."

Clara burst out laughing. "You made that up."

"Maybe." He dipped his bread in the pool of olive oil on his plate. "If I thought it would scare her into leaving me alone, I'd set Tatters on her."

"I think even Tatters is afraid of her." Clara poured a dash of balsamic vinegar into the oil on her plate and watched it form tiny puddles. "Speaking of whom, I think I've come up with a solution to your problem. That's if you'll agree."

Rick looked as if he were about to hug her. "You have? I'll agree to anything if it will mean taking care of that dog."

Clara took a deep breath. "Well, I've been thinking about it all day, and I think this might work. I don't have to be at the bookstore until noon, and my mother gets home from the library around four, so that just leaves a few hours for Tatters to be alone."

Amazement transfixed Rick's face. "Are you saying you want Tatters to live with you?"

Clara gulped. Now that she'd actually spoken the words, the reality was beginning to sink in. "I . . . er . . . think so. I haven't actually discussed it with my mother yet, but she loves dogs and I'm sure—"

"No! I can't let you do that." Rick reached out and covered her hand with his own, making her forget everything except his gray eyes peering earnestly into hers. "You have no idea what you'd be taking on. That dog is totally unmanageable, and he'd wreck your house the first time you left him alone. Trust me."

Whenever someone told Clara she couldn't do something, it only made her more determined. "I'm sure I can handle him. He'd have a permanent home, and you'd be very welcome to see him whenever you like, take him for walks, or keep him overnight if you wanted."

He studied her face for so long she became

uncomfortable. Drawing her hand from his, she said, a little stiffly, "Of course, if you don't think he'd be happy . . ."

"Happy? He'd be ecstatic! So would I. I'm just wondering why you'd want to do this. Not that I'm not grateful, of course, but—"

"I love dogs, too." She wasn't quite sure of her motives, either, but she wasn't about to admit that. Even to herself. That train of thought could be too dangerous. "Tatters is a sweetheart," she added as Rick continued to look doubtful. "He just needs a little attention, that's all. I know you do your best, but you're so busy with the store all the time and you must be tired when you get home . . ."

Rick grinned. "Thanks for making excuses for me." He sat back in his chair. "The truth is, the dog reminds me of some things I'd rather forget. I've tried to get past that, but it's tough."

"Oh." Now she didn't know what to say.

"Anyway, if you're serious—"

Yes, she was serious. No matter what Jessie said, Tatters was coming home with her. With everything else Rick was dealing with right now, he didn't need the emotional upheaval his dog presented. "I'll talk to my mother tonight, and if it's okay with you, I'll come over and pick up Tatters in the morning."

"Assuming your mother agrees."

"She'll agree," Clara promised him, with more confidence than she felt. It was either that, or she'd find somewhere else to live.

"In that case, I'll have Tatters' things packed up and ready to go." He smiled, looking boyish in his relief. "I have to admit, it would be a huge load off my mind. With all that's going on, things are a bit uncertain. It'll be easier to handle if I've only got myself to worry about." He raised his wineglass. "Here's to a really good friend. Thank you."

She touched glasses with him. "You're welcome. It'll be fun."

"I don't know about that." He took a sip of his wine. "Promise me, if he gets to be too much for you, you'll send him back to me, okay?"

"I don't think that will happen, but I'll promise anyway." She sipped her wine, her thoughts on Rick's words. *It'll be easier to handle if I've only got myself to worry about.* It was obvious he was worried about the outcome of the murder investigation. She could hardly blame him. Being the chief suspect had to be devastating. The Web was full of stories about people being convicted of crimes they didn't commit. If only there was something she could do to help.

As if in answer, the Sense spoke clearly in her ear. *Look for the motive.*

She must have had an odd expression on her face. Rick tilted his head on one side. "Heartburn?"

"What?" She blinked at him, then shook her head. "Oh! No." She uttered a light laugh. "I was just thinking about the murder. Once the police identify the victim, it should help take their attention off you, since you've never seen the guy before."

"It should. It doesn't mean it will. I have a feeling the mayor has already decided I'm guilty. I'm just wondering how long it will take him to convince Dan of that."

He was echoing Roberta's words, making Clara feel even more concerned for him. "You're innocent," she said softly. "Hang on to that. The truth will come out eventually."

His smile was bleak. "I hope you're right. So, what did you think of the farmer's market? Is it worth a visit?"

He had deliberately changed the subject, and she was quick to respond. "It was crowded, and hot. I ended up coming home with just a bag of cherries. I guess I should have gone earlier in the morning."

"There's a very big farmer's market in Mittleford." He went on to describe it, and the conversation drifted from there to the benefits of organic produce and then to her favorite New York restaurants.

All too soon it was time to leave. As Clara led the way out to the parking lot, she rehearsed how she would tell her mother to expect an addition to the family. She could only hope that her decision to adopt Tatters wouldn't turn into a major battle.

"Thank you for dinner," she said as Rick paused with her at her car. "I really enjoyed it."

She couldn't see his face too clearly in the darkness, but he sounded a little remorseful when he answered. "Even though we spent most of it discussing my problems?"

"Hey, that's what friends are for, aren't they?" She opened the car door and climbed inside. "Everything's going to turn out all right. I know it."

He ducked his head to look at her. "Thanks for the vote of confidence. It means a lot to me. And thanks for taking on the brute. I hope he doesn't cause you too much trouble."

"You worry too much." She started the engine. "We'll be fine."

He stood back and lifted his hand in farewell as she closed the door.

As she drove out of the parking lot, she glanced in her side mirror. He was still standing there, watching her leave as she turned the corner and drove away.

4

When Clara arrived home, Jessie pounced on her the moment she walked through the door. "How was your dinner? Where did you go? What did you have?"

Clara answered all her questions, waiting for the one she knew Jessie was dying to ask.

"So, who did you have dinner with tonight?" Jessie looked put out. "You never used to be so secretive. You used to tell me everything without me having to drag it out of you. I don't know what happened to you in New York to change you so much."

It was a complaint her mother had repeated too many times to count. As usual, Clara ignored it. "I had dinner with Rick Sanders, if you must know."

Jessie followed her into the living room. "Rick Sanders? I thought you weren't interested in him."

"I'm not. Not in that way." Clara flung herself down on the couch, resigned to the imminent confrontation. "It was more of a business meeting."

Jessie sat down on the armchair opposite her, eyes wide with astonishment. "He offered you a *job*?"

Clara sighed. "No, Mother. I offered to adopt his dog."

She paused, expecting an outburst of protest. She wasn't disappointed.

"You *what*? You're joking. You have to be. When do you have time to look after a dog? Where in the world would we put it? What kind of dog? Are you out of your *mind*?"

Clara waited for her mother to pause for breath before saying mildly, "Rick was going to send him to the pound. I couldn't bear the thought of him being put down, so I sort of rescued him. His name is Tatters." She leaned forward. "He's adorable, Mom. You'll love him."

Jessie's cheeks still burned with annoyance. "I can't believe you promised to adopt a *dog* without consulting me. What in the world has gotten into you? You never used to be so impulsive and inconsiderate."

Gritting her teeth, Clara sat up and took a deep breath. "I didn't promise Rick anything. I said I would take Tatters if you agreed."

"Oh." Jessie looked somewhat mollified. "Well, I suppose we could discuss it. I need some time to think about it first."

"I said I'd pick him up tomorrow." Seeing her mother's eyebrows draw together again, she quickly added, "If you agree, that is." She leaned forward again. "You don't really want to be responsible for having a beautiful, loving, gentle dog put down, do you?" She shut down the vision of Tatters lunging across the road in happy pursuit of Roberta Prince.

"Of course not, but—"

"Great! Then I'll pick him up tomorrow." She got up from the couch, hoping to put an end to the conversation.

She was halfway across the room when her mother said, "I suppose you heard the latest news about Rick Sanders?"

Clara paused at the door. "What news is that? I've heard so many things that aren't true, I'm not sure I want to hear any more."

"Well, you might want to hear this. Betsy was here a little while ago and she told me."

Clara rolled her eyes. Betsy lived next door and was always sharing the latest gossip with Jessie. "So, what did she have to say?"

"The man who was found dead in Rick's truck? Well, it turns out he was in Rick's hardware store on the day he was killed. John Halloran recognized his picture on TV and called Dan."

Clara's stomach did a little nosedive. "That doesn't mean anything."

"Then why did Rick say he'd never seen the man before?"

Good question. Clara shut out the voices. "He was probably somewhere else when the man came in."

"Maybe, but you have to admit, things are really piling

up against Rick. Are you sure you want to be associated with him right now?"

Clara frowned. "I'm not *associated* with anyone. He's my friend and I'm simply adopting his dog, that's all. Even if I were interested in him, which I'm not, I wouldn't be taking any notice of all the ugly rumors flying around that have absolutely no basis and are causing the poor man unnecessary worry and misery. People should be ashamed of themselves, spreading around such vicious idle gossip."

Jessie raised her eyebrows. "For someone who professes to have no personal interest in the man, you are making a great deal of fuss in his defense."

Clara let out her exasperation in an explosive grunt. "I'm going to bed. Good-night." Stomping down the hallway to her bedroom, she tried to rationalize her ill-temper. Was she angry because Rick was being victimized without due cause? Or was she, perhaps, mad at her mother for suggesting that her interest in Rick went a little deeper than mere friendship?

If it was the latter, then she was in trouble. Because the only way that would make her mad was if there were some truth to the insinuation. And that was something she didn't want to explore.

She awoke in the middle of the night, perspiration dampening her forehead. At first she thought she'd been dreaming, but now she was wide awake, and the vision was still clear in her mind.

She saw the shadow of a man, backing away from

another figure until he was stopped by the wall behind him. It was dark, but she could make out the two men, struggling for possession of something that glinted in the lights of a passing car. One of the men broke free and tried to run, but the other was on him, pounding him with the weapon in his hand until his victim fell to the ground.

She sat up, struggling to see the faces, but it was too dark and blurry to make them out. One thing she was certain of—neither man was Rick. One was too short, the other too chubby. Then the vision vanished, leaving her shivering in the cool draft of the air-conditioning.

The following morning she got up early and was ready to leave by the time her mother came down to breakfast. She was halfway out the door when Jessie called out to her, "If you bring that dog home, I just hope you know what you're doing."

So did she, she told herself as she climbed into her car. She really hadn't given the whole idea enough thought. It was one thing inviting a dog into her mother's house. Quite another when that dog was the size of a small pony. She hoped Rick would have enough dog food to keep Tatters happy until she could get to the pet store, or wherever he bought the stuff. She couldn't remember seeing a pet store in Finn's Harbor.

By the time she'd parked her car and walked up to Parson's Hardware, she was having second thoughts about the whole situation. What if her powers weren't strong enough to control the dog? What if they weren't there when she needed them as had happened so often in the past? What if Tatters totally destroyed her mother's home?

Closing her eyes, she made an effort to dismiss her fears. Other people had control of their dogs without the benefit of the Quinn Sense. So could she. All she needed was a little time to work with Tatters.

She reached the door of the hardware store just in time to see the big dog bounding across the shop floor, his tail sweeping a row of plastic flowerpots off the shelf. They rolled across the floor toward her as Tatters flew past her out the door.

John Halloran stumbled over to her, bellowing something she couldn't understand. She didn't wait to find out. Spinning around, she lunged after the dog. He darted across the street ahead of her and plunked his rear end down on the doorstep of Jordan's Stationer's.

Unfortunately Roberta Prince was just coming out the door. She tripped over Tatters, tottered on her high heels down the step, and ended up in a heap on the sidewalk. Her howl of outrage could be heard all the way down the hill to the harbor.

Clara reached her as she was climbing to her feet, one hand brushing dust from her pale lilac pants while shaking her fist at Tatters. "You disgusting animal! You should be locked up in a kennel. You're a menace on the street." She advanced on the dog. "Get off my doorstep. *Shoo!*"

Tatters sat panting, his tongue hanging out the side of his mouth almost as if he were grinning at her.

Clara leapt forward and grabbed his collar. "Are you all right? You're not hurt?"

"No, but it's a miracle I'm not." Roberta glared at the dog. "Get that beast off my property. If he comes back again, I swear I'll call the pound and have him picked up."

"He won't be back." Clara patted his silky head. "I'm taking him home with me."

Roberta stared at her. "Does Rick know that?"

"Of course he does." Clara glanced across the street. "We arranged it last night."

"Last night?" Roberta's face turned a light pink. "I didn't know you were on *those* kind of terms with Rick."

Clara rolled her eyes. Why was everyone so quick to link her with Rick Sanders? "I'm not on any terms with Rick. This is a business arrangement, that's all."

"Oh, he's *paying* you to take care of the dog."

Her demeaning tone set Clara's teeth on edge. Deciding to let it go, she muttered, "I have to get him back to the store." She tugged the dog's collar. "Come on, Tatters. Good boy."

I'm not going back there.

Clara jerked her hand from the collar. She'd never felt comfortable on the rare occasion she'd read someone's thoughts, and although she'd suspected for some time that dogs understood what she said, this was the first time that she'd ever read a dog's mind. She glanced at Roberta, but the other woman was gazing down the street with her usual bored expression.

Clara scowled at Tatters. Just great. Now the dog was speaking in her head. That's all she needed. She took hold of the collar again. "You're going back there whether you like it or not."

Tatters yawned, and stayed where he was.

"I suppose Rick had to do something about that beast," Roberta said, "now that he won't be around to take care of things himself."

Still shaken by what had just happened, Clara stared at her. "What do you mean by that?"

Roberta shrugged. "It's all over the news. He's been arrested." She started down the street calling over her shoulder, "I thought you would have known that, considering your *business* arrangement."

Clara didn't even bother to answer her. She laid her hand on the back of Tatters' neck. "Let's go," she said firmly. *"Now."*

Tatters shifted away from her, turned his head and licked her hand.

Clara bent down and looked him in the eye. "Listen, Buster, if you don't come with me this instant, I will take you to the pound. Do you know what happens to dogs who are left at the pound?"

Tatters whined, got up and started across the street.

If she hadn't been so anxious about Rick, she would have been pleased with her small victory. Rushing behind Tatters into the store, she almost collided with John, who had apparently been watching her from the doorway.

"Thank God," he muttered as the dog fled past him.

"Rick would have killed me if anything had happened to that stupid animal."

Clara glared at him. "Why didn't you tell me Rick had been arrested?"

"You didn't exactly give me time. Besides, he hasn't been arrested. He's being held for questioning. It was all on the news. I thought you would have heard it by now."

Clara made a mental note to change the channel on her car radio. "What happened? Why now?"

John dropped his gaze and straightened his glasses. "I recognized the photo of the murder victim. I told Dan he was here in the store the morning he was killed and that Rick had served him." He shook his head. "How was I to know that Rick had sworn he'd never seen the guy before? Dan and Deputy Tim Rossi got here soon after Rick opened this morning and took him down to the station. Rick called me to come in, and now I'm stuck here taking care of the store until he either shuts it down or gets someone in here to help."

"That's ridiculous."

"I know. I don't have time to work all day in here."

"No, I mean about taking him down to the station. He probably just didn't recognize the guy, that's all. I don't remember every stranger that comes into the bookstore." Clara briefly closed her eyes as the vision she'd had that morning popped into her mind. *If only I could see their faces. Maybe if I really concentrated . . .* When she opened her eyes again, John was staring at her as if she'd said something shocking. "What?"

John shook his head. "I dunno. You had that weird look on your face, like you know something no one else does."

She gave him a tight smile. "Maybe I do."

"Well, if I were you, I'd be mighty careful about sharing it." His eyes gleamed at her through his glasses. "You could end up getting into serious trouble."

She frowned, wondering what he was insinuating. Just then Tatters barked, snatching her attention away from John. The dog sat by the counter, his tail sweeping the floor as he clenched a plastic garden frog between his teeth.

John let out a howl of protest and rushed over to him. Taking hold of the frog, he tried to drag it out of Tatters' mouth. Tatters growled, making John let go and jump back into the shelves behind him.

Clara closed her eyes as hammers, chisels and screwdrivers crashed to the floor. Tatters whined and fled behind the counter. John swore, and began picking up the fallen tools, muttering something under his breath that mercifully Clara couldn't hear.

"Er . . . do you know if Rick brought any dog supplies with him this morning?" she said, edging toward the end of the counter.

"In the back room," John grunted. He stood up and packed some screwdrivers back on the shelf. "He said to take what you need."

"Thanks." Clara darted through the door that led to the back room. She saw the huge bag of dry dog food and hauled it into her arms. Spotting a paper sack on a nearby chair, she peeked inside. There were two dog bowls, a leash, a couple of packages of treats, a chewed-up tennis ball and a large rawhide bone. Everything a dog could want.

After carrying everything to the front door, she called out to John, who was still picking up and sorting the tools on the shelf. "I'm going to get my car and park it in the loading zone."

He answered her with a wave, and she dashed out the door and down the hill. She still had an hour or so before she was due at the bookstore. Enough time to get Tatters home and settled before she had to leave him.

It occurred to her that she should have waited until her next day off before bringing the dog into his new home. It was too late now, however. Besides, if Rick did end up in jail after his questioning, there'd be no one to look after Tatters.

He doesn't belong in jail. Startled, she closed her mind to the voices. She didn't need them to tell her that. Rick was innocent, and somehow she had to help him.

Right then, however, her first priority was to get Tatters home and settled. Then she'd tackle the problem of Rick's possible arrest.

John grudgingly helped her haul the dog food and supplies into the trunk of her car, and even located the leash that Rick had shoved under the counter. Tatters seemed excited about the prospect of a car ride and bounded onto the backseat, where he sat with his nose pressed to the window while Clara started the engine and pulled away from the store.

To her huge relief, the dog sat on his haunches all the way home, though the minute she parked the car at the curb he jumped up and started barking—little short yelps that Clara recognized as anxiety as she opened the door.

He would have leapt past her had she not grabbed his collar and hung on with all her strength while she talked to him in soothing tones. "It's all right, big boy. You're home. You're gonna be all right now."

It took a while but gradually Tatters stopped quivering and yelping and allowed her to lead him out of the car and up the path to the front door.

It took her another hour to get him fed and settled down. After removing everything breakable in her room, she coaxed him onto her bed. Leaning down to look him in the eye, she said firmly, "You are to stay here, on this bed, until Mom gets home."

She waited, anxiously holding her breath in case she heard his voice in her head again. To her relief, he merely whined, and moved his tail slowly back and forth. Feeling reassured, she added, "She will let you out in the yard when she gets home and she'll feed you. You are to be on your best behavior, is that understood?"

Tatters lifted his head and licked her nose.

Satisfied, Clara rubbed his ears and patted his head. After turning on her small TV, she left the room and closed the door. She waited just long enough to reassure herself he wasn't going berserk in there, and then called her mother.

Jessie sounded worried when she answered. "They've arrested Rick Sanders for that murder," she said. "I don't think you should be having anything to do with him. I hope you haven't brought that dog home. I won't have a murderer's dog in my home. I wouldn't feel safe."

Clara took a deep breath and let it out slowly before answering her. "Rick is not a murderer, and he hasn't been arrested. He's just being questioned, that's all. Someone has to take care of Tatters while he's at the station. The dog is in my room." She gave her mother brief instructions to let Tatters out in the yard and feed him.

"Does he have to stay in the yard until you get home?" Jessie asked doubtfully. "Won't he be lonely out there, poor little thing?"

Clara felt guilty. Her mother had no idea she'd be dealing with a large dog. Better she didn't know until she actually met Tatters. Hopefully the dog would win over Jessie. Clara closed her eyes and prayed that Tatters would behave until she got home. If not, she'd have more than a hysterical mother to deal with.

Feeling decidedly uneasy, she drove back to Main Street and parked the car. The slight breeze from the ocean did nothing to cool her face as she trudged up the hill for the second time that day. She already felt as if she'd worked a full day, and she hadn't even started her shift at the bookstore yet.

Stephanie was behind the counter when Clara walked in, followed by a couple of giggling teenagers who promptly disappeared down one of the aisles.

"I suppose you heard the news," she said as Clara tucked her purse on the shelf under the counter. "Rick's been arrested."

"He has *not* been arrested! Why is everyone so darn quick to convict him?"

She'd spoken more sharply than she'd intended, and Stephanie raised her eyebrows. "*Sor*-ry! Roberta said he'd been arrested. I didn't know she had it wrong."

Clara sighed. "You should know better than to listen to Roberta Prince. She exaggerates everything."

Stephanie took Clara's arm. "You look frazzled. Come on down to the Nook and we'll have a cup of coffee. Molly can take care of the counter for a while."

Clara followed her cousin down the aisle where Molly was stacking books on a shelf. Catching sight of Clara, the young woman bounced over to her. "Did you hear the news? I can't believe they arrested—"

Both cousins spoke at once. "He's not been arrested!"

Molly blinked. "Oh, I thought . . ."

She let her voice trail off as Clara glared at her. "From now on, if anyone mentions the word *arrest* in my presence, expect to get an earful, is that clear?"

Molly nodded and glanced at Stephanie.

"I need you at the counter," Stephanie said, nudging Clara to go forward. "We'll be in the Nook if anyone wants us."

"Got it!" Molly darted off, no doubt glad to be out of the line of fire.

Clara flung herself down on a chair in the Nook and rubbed her forehead with her fingers.

"Headache?" Stephanie handed her a mug of steaming coffee.

"A pounder. It's been quite a morning."

"Yeah, I saw you earlier. What on earth were you doing with that dog?"

Clara filled her in, making her laugh more than once as she related the events of the morning.

"I bet Aunt Jessie will have a screaming fit when she sees Tatters," Stephanie said when Clara finished her story.

"I'm just hoping she doesn't freak out when she opens my bedroom door." Clara tried not to visualize Tatters tearing through the house, leaving a trail of broken knick-knacks behind him.

Stephanie leaned back in her chair. "Reminds me of the time you found that poor little dog in the woods. You took it home, and Aunt Jessie wouldn't let it in the house because it was running alive with fleas."

Clara smiled. "I remember. We kept that puppy for days in the woodshed on McAllister's farm."

"Until Mr. McAllister found out and chased us out of there." Stephanie stared into her coffee mug. "I remember how you held that dog in your lap and talked to it like it was a child. You kept listening as if it was talking to you and you could understand every word it said. Then you got up, said you knew where it lived, and we took it to that house near the woods."

"I was right. That little girl cried when we gave her back her puppy."

"That dog told you where it lived."

Clara shifted on her chair and put the mug down on the table at her side. "It was just a lucky guess. I pretended it told me. We were kids. We were always pretending things. If we weren't sailing the high seas with a bunch of pirates we were flying on a magic carpet to Aladdin's castle."

"Or pretending to be fortune-tellers. We couldn't wait to get the Quinn Sense so we could tell fortunes for real."

"Yeah, well that didn't turn out to be nearly as exciting as we imagined."

"I wouldn't know." Stephanie gave her a hard look. "What are you going to do about Rick?"

Clara raised her eyebrows. "What should I be doing?"

"I mean, if he's guilty—if he really did kill that guy—"

"Stephanie Quinn Dowd! How can you say that? You know Rick as well as I do. He could never do something like that."

Stephanie looked worried. "Clara, aren't you just a little prejudiced? I know you like the guy. How can you be so sure he didn't do it?"

Clara pinched her lips. "I know. Just leave it at that."

Stephanie stared at her, her expression slowly changing from doubt to recognition. "The Quinn Sense. It was the Sense that told you, right?" She slapped the arm of her chair. "Darn it, I wish I could do that! It's not fair. Why should you get the powers and not me? We're practically sisters, for heaven's sake! Most of our family has it, why can't I?"

"Shhh!" Clara looked around in alarm. "You know how I feel about that. I don't want anyone to know I have it."

"Sorry." Stephanie leaned forward. "I was right, though, wasn't I? That's how come you're so sure Rick is innocent."

"I believe he's innocent because I know him. Well enough to know he's not a murderer." Clara paused, knowing that what she was about to say had been in her mind ever since she'd heard that Rick was a suspect. "I'm going to do my best to prove it," she said quietly.

Stephanie frowned. "Have you forgotten what happened when you helped clear Molly's name?"

"No, of course not. But Rick needs my help. I don't see anyone else rushing to his aid."

"He has a lawyer, hasn't he?"

"Yes, but lawyers are interested in proving their clients' innocence, not tracking down the real murderer."

"Isn't that what the police department is supposed to do?"

Clara sighed. "Yes, they are. Dan is a good cop, and I know he's doing his best to find out the truth. But it's like we said when Molly was a suspect. People don't like talking to the cops. They'll talk to us. Someone out there knows what really happened. All we have to do is find him."

Stephanie's eyes gleamed. "And there's always the Quinn Sense."

"You know how erratic that can be."

"It's helped before."

"Maybe. But I'm not going to rely on it. I'm just going to ask questions and hope someone comes up with the right answer."

"But if the Sense can help?"

Clara paused a long moment before answering. "Much as I hate to admit it, it could come in handy."

Stephanie sat up. "All right! Since you're determined to do this, I'm going to help you."

Clara smiled. "I thought you might."

"As long as you bear in mind that I'm the ideas person. You're the one who does the legwork."

"Of course. I wouldn't have it any other way."

"And we don't tell George what we're doing. He'd kill me if he knew we were chasing after another murderer."

"I wouldn't dream of telling him." Clara hesitated. "Unless it's a dire emergency."

Stephanie frowned again. "Promise me you won't do anything rash. We must never forget that this could be dangerous."

"Absolutely." Clara leaned forward. "Thanks, Steffie. It'll be easier if there's two of us."

"What about Molly?"

"What about her?"

"You know she'd want in on this. After all, we helped

find the real killer when she was a suspect. I know she'll want to do what she can to clear Rick's name."

Clara thought about it for a moment before nodding. "If we need her, we'll ask for her help. For now, though, I'd like to keep this just between us."

Stephanie raised her coffee mug. "To the Quinn cousins, and our quest."

Clara picked up her own mug and tapped it against her cousin's. "To success." She was about to drink when the familiar sensation washed over her. The voice spoke so loudly in her ear she thought Stephanie might have heard it. *Beware of the blind alley. Danger lies in the gutter.*

Her expression must have given her thoughts away, as her cousin stared at her. "What? What is it? Have you thought of something?"

Clara sighed. "More like heard something." She repeated the words.

Stephanie leaned forward, eyes gleaming with excitement. "The Sense told you that? What does it mean?"

"I wish I knew." Clara took a sip of her coffee and put down her mug, the strange message still buzzing in her head. "Wait." She met Stephanie's gaze. "I think I know what the voices are telling me. What are you doing tonight?"

5

Stephanie waited until George had changed into shorts and a T-shirt and was settled in his favorite chair before delivering her announcement. "I need you to babysit tonight."

George sipped his beer and regarded her over the rim of his glass. "Going somewhere?"

"Clara and I are going bowling."

George choked, spilling beer down the side of his glass. "*Bowling?* You haven't been bowling since we got married."

Stephanie shrugged. "Clara wanted to go and asked me if I'd go with her."

George's thick red eyebrows drew together across his nose. "Does this have anything to do with Rick Sanders being arrested?"

Stephanie opened her eyes wide. "What? Rick has been arrested? I thought he was just being held for questioning."

George put down his glass and crossed his arms. "Whatever. You know what I mean."

"I have no idea what you mean." Stephanie struggled to avoid telling an outright lie. "Clara suggested we go bowling tonight, and I thought it might be fun, that's all."

"Uh-huh. Seems to me that whenever you two get together, something bad happens."

"Whatever are you talking about?" Stephanie heard the raised voices of her children floating down the stairs. "All we want to do is have a little fun. You know Clara doesn't have friends here yet. She's getting bored sitting at home at night." She started walking toward the stairs. "It's hard on her living back here after being used to big-city life." She put a foot on the bottom step and yelled at the top of her voice. "*Michael! Olivia!* Stop fighting this instant. *Ethan?* Where are you? Stop those kids from fighting. *Now!*"

Ethan's eleven-year-old voice rose above the shouts of his younger siblings. "Aw, *Mom*. I'm doing homework."

Stephanie glared up at her invisible son. "No, you're not. It's summertime. You don't have homework. Drag yourself away from Facebook for five minutes and find out what those two are fighting about."

Returning to George, she muttered, "Is it too much to ask to have an hour or so to myself?"

George rolled his eyes. "All right, all right. Go

bowling. Just don't come crying to me if you get into trouble with Dan for interfering in police business."

Stephanie dropped her jaw. "Why on earth would I want to do that?"

"You've done it before."

"That was different."

George stood up. "Stay out of this, Stephanie. I don't want to have to identify your dead body in the morgue. Who would I get to iron my undies if you're not around?"

Stephanie uttered a dry laugh. "Don't worry, there's no chance of that." She couldn't help feeling a bit apprehensive as she hurried into the kitchen to start preparing dinner. She consoled herself with the thought that she and Clara had agreed that at the first sign of real danger they would hand everything over to Dan. That's if they could find out anything useful.

Dan and his deputies were far more experienced at tracking down a murderer, but the cousins had one thing that Dan didn't. The Quinn Sense. Already it had pointed them toward the bowling alley with the cryptic message Clara had received. *Beware of the blind alley. Danger lies in the gutter.* Stephanie was impressed that Clara had seemed to instantly know what the words meant.

True, the Sense was unpredictable, and not always there when needed, but Stephanie had a lot more faith in it than her cousin did, and felt reasonably sure that it would warn them if they were getting into more trouble than they could handle.

With that firmly in mind, she pushed the uneasy thoughts out of her head and concentrated on making the salad.

———

Clara arrived home from the bookstore full of apprehension. She'd been waiting all afternoon and evening for her mother to call and scream about some disaster caused by Tatters. When the call didn't come, she didn't know whether to be relieved or worried by the unexpected silence.

Standing at the front door with her ear pressed against it, she listened for any sign of a commotion inside. Hearing nothing, she fitted her key into the lock and turned it. As she opened the door, she heard voices from the TV and thought she caught the sound of a low *Woof!* from the direction of the living room.

She paused, waiting for the onslaught of furry paws. When no sign of Tatters materialized, her first thought was that her mother had done something dreadful to the dog. Or vice versa.

Rushing into the living room, she felt a wave of relief at the sight of her mother sitting calmly on her chair in front of the blaring TV. That quickly changed to astonishment when she saw Tatters curled up at Jessie's feet, nose on his paws. His big brown eyes watched Clara as she crossed the room toward him.

Jessie looked up as Clara approached. "Oh, there you are. I've left a casserole in the fridge if you want to heat it up."

Clara heard the words but was too concerned to pay attention to them. "What have you done to Tatters?" She dropped on her knees by the side of the dog. Tatters yawned and sat up.

Jessie glanced down at her. "What? Oh, nothing much. We had a nice talk, that's all. He was a bit boisterous when I first let him out, but after I picked myself up off the floor, I gave him a lecture and he soon settled down."

Clara let out her breath. Having been on the blunt end of her mother's lectures, she could almost feel sorry for Tatters. She fondled the dog's ears. "Did you have a nice afternoon, then, boy?"

Tatters whined and licked her nose.

"I do think you could have warned me," Jessie said, getting up from the chair. "I was expecting a little puppy, not a full-grown Bigfoot. It was rather a shock to find myself on the floor with two huge hairy paws on my chest."

"Sorry." Clara got to her feet. "I knew you could handle him, though. You always were better with animals than people."

Jessie looked offended. "What does that mean?"

Clara smiled. "Nothing. I just meant you have a way with animals, that's all. It looks as if you've got Tatters totally under control."

"Well, you never know. One has to keep a stern eye on animals. They can be difficult when they're upset."

Like some humans she knew, Clara thought, but resisted the temptation to say so. "Well then, I guess you won't mind keeping an eye on him this evening." She glanced at the clock. "I just came home to change. I'm meeting Steffie at the bowling alley in a few minutes."

Jessie stared at her in dismay. "What about dinner?"

"I'll grab something out there." Clara headed for the hallway.

"But I wanted to tell you about—"

Clara waved a hand at her. "It'll have to wait. I'll be late if I don't get going." She dashed down the hallway and into her room before her mother could argue.

Ten minutes later she was ready to leave. Her mother met her in the hallway, holding up her hand to prevent her passing.

"I just wanted to tell you that the murder victim has been identified."

Clara paused in the act of opening the front door. Spinning around, she demanded, "Who is it?"

"I can't remember his name. Something Polish, I think." Jessie frowned. "He worked in construction or something in Portland. Apparently he was here on vacation and was staying at one of those dreadful motels on the coast road."

"Who identified him?"

"The manager of the motel. He didn't see a photo of the victim until late this afternoon when he saw the front page of the newspaper. Apparently he doesn't watch much TV."

"Do they know who killed him?"

Jessie gave her a pitying look. "They're still saying

that they have no suspects in custody but that Rick Sanders is helping in their investigation. Carson Dexter was there again, demanding the police make an arrest. He more or less hinted that Rick should be arrested for the murder."

Clara grunted in disgust. "Carson Dexter is an idiot." She opened the door and stepped outside. "I won't be late."

Jessie moved forward to stand in the doorway. "Be careful, Clara. You have always been too trusting, you know."

Clara's mouth twisted in a wry smile. "Not anymore, Mother. Never again. Believe me." Without waiting for an answer, she fled down the path to her car.

Stephanie had already arrived and was waiting in the doorway when Clara parked in front of the bowling alley. "We're not really going to play, are we?" she asked anxiously as Clara led the way into the foyer. "I haven't bowled since my teens and even then I was known as the gutter-ball queen."

The clatter of falling pins and the thumping of a heavy metal band made it hard to hear her. "Let's get something to eat." Clara grabbed her arm and pulled her toward the bar. It was relatively quiet in there, and she chose a table in the far corner, away from the door.

"I've already eaten dinner," Stephanie protested as Clara reached for the menu.

"Then just have a glass of wine." Clara scanned the items and decided on a chicken Caesar wrap.

A young woman wearing jeans and a low-cut tank top

ambled up to the table and flipped over a page of her notepad. "What can I get you?"

Her tone of voice suggested she could care less, and Clara had a fleeting moment of nostalgia for the trendy New York bistro where she'd enjoyed so many delicious lunches. She ordered the wrap and two glasses of wine, then sat back to scan the bar.

Several men were seated at the long counter, and the two bartenders were busy filling beer glasses. Clara watched the man and woman behind the counter for a long moment, then leaned forward and spoke in a low voice just loud enough for Stephanie to hear. "I think we need to talk to one of the bartenders."

Stephanie glanced over at the counter. "Do you think they know something?"

"I don't know. I'm just guessing it's a good place to start."

"Didn't the Sense tell you where to start?"

Clara sighed. "No, it didn't. All I know is that being here will help us find out something useful."

"Okay." Stephanie studied the hustling bartenders for a moment. "Which one? They both look busy."

"Both of them. We'll take one each."

"What will we talk about?"

"The murder, of course. Just listen to anything they say and try to get as much out of them as possible."

Now Stephanie looked worried. "I'm not good at this. You usually do all the talking and asking."

Clara smiled. "I'm not good at it, either, but between us we should get something we can use."

Her cousin was unconvinced. "We're not very good detectives."

"We're not trying to be detectives. We're just trying to help a friend, that's all."

Stephanie's frown vanished. "Ah well, when you put it that way, I—"

She broke off as their server slapped two glasses of wine down between them. "Your wrap will be along in a minute," she said, and sauntered off to the next table.

Stephanie dragged a paper napkin out of the holder and mopped up the spilt wine. "I should make her pay for that," she muttered.

"I guess you heard that the murder victim has been identified?"

Stephanie nodded. "On the news. The mayor was on there, too. He made it sound like Rick was guilty."

"So I heard." Clara played with her wineglass, twisting it around so the light glimmered on the swirling liquid. "He's just anxious to get an arrest. I read somewhere that he's planning to run for governor in the next election."

"So that's why he's making such a big fuss about the murder. He wants credit for getting it solved fast." Stephanie took a sip of her wine and winced. "Ugh. This tastes like it's been watered down."

"It probably has." Clara spotted the server strolling

toward them once more, carrying a plate. "Here comes my wrap."

"I hope it's better than the wine."

They were both silent until the young woman had left, then Stephanie murmured, "So what do you think about the victim—Frank Toski or something? They said he was a construction worker here on vacation, but doesn't it seem strange that he would be here by himself?"

Clara shrugged. "I dunno. There must be lots of people who go on vacation by themselves."

"I suppose. He just didn't look like the type who would want to spend a vacation alone in a town like Finn's Harbor."

Clara bit into her wrap and mulled over what her cousin had just said. "If you're right," she said, "then he must have come here for a reason."

"Exactly." Stephanie beamed. "So, if we could just find out why he was really here, then we might be able to find out who killed him."

Clara raised her glass at her cousin. "I always said you were the brains in the family."

"I'm the ideas person, remember?"

"How could I forget? Some of your ideas have had memorable consequences."

Stephanie raised her chin. "Like what?"

"Like the time you thought it would be a good idea to teach old Nellie Hatcher's cat to swim."

"I wasn't going to teach him to swim. I just wanted to be sure he could. Nellie had that big pond in her yard, and the cat was always trying to catch the goldfish in it. I was worried he would drown if he fell in."

"So you took him into the *ocean* to see if he could swim?"

Stephanie shrugged. "What did I know? I was only six. I meant to hold on to him in case he sank, but he jumped out of my arms when the first wave hit."

Clara shook her head. "I remember. We both nearly drowned trying to rescue him."

"He got back to the beach before we did."

"Well, I guess you found out he could swim, and better than we could at the time."

Stephanie grinned. "Our parents made us take swimming lessons after that, so something good came out of it. Not all of my ideas ended up in disaster."

"Okay, so now come up with an idea of why our guy was here."

Stephanie's forehead creased in concentration. "Looking for a job? Construction work is in the pits everywhere. Maybe he decided to relocate here to find work."

"In Finn's Harbor? I haven't heard of any construction projects going on around here. Have you?"

Stephanie shook her head. "Okay, he was meeting someone down here. A woman."

Clara grinned. "Always the romantic."

"It's possible."

"If that's so, why hasn't the woman come forward? Or anyone else, come to that. If he was here to meet someone, they must have seen his picture in the paper."

"That's a good point." She thought about it for a moment. "I guess whoever he was going to meet didn't want the cops to know about it."

"Exactly." Clara lifted her wineglass. "Since he was apparently killed in this parking lot, he was probably meeting that person here in the bowling alley."

"They must have been up to some funny business, then." She had a pained look on her face as she watched Clara swallow the wine. "Pretty bad, isn't it?"

"It's not good." Clara set down her glass. "So, what we need to do is find out who he was meeting here that night. I'm hoping the bartenders can tell us that."

Stephanie frowned. "Wouldn't they have already told the police?"

"Maybe not. Or maybe they didn't tell them everything. There's only one way to find out."

"So which one do you want to talk to?" Stephanie peered at the bartenders over the rim of her glass. "I don't know either one of them. Do you?"

Clara laughed. "I've been gone for ten years. You know the people here better than I do."

Stephanie shook her head. "A lot of people have left since you went away, and more people are moving in all the time. This bowling alley has only been open a couple of years. I've never been in here before."

"Ah well, the good thing is, the bartenders won't know who we are, either. It might make it easier to get answers."

"Unless they've been in the bookstore." Stephanie studied the man and woman behind the counter for a few more seconds. "Nope. They don't look like readers to me."

"Then let's get it over with. We'll go over there, order a drink, and hope they've got time to talk." Clara pushed her plate away and drained her glass. "Remember, don't let on you know Rick personally. Just say you heard the news on the TV and you're curious about it."

"Won't it seem odd to them that both of us are asking questions about the murder?"

Clara smiled. "Probably, but hopefully not before they've given us the answers we want."

"Okay, let's go." Stephanie fluffed her fair hair back from her face, squared her shoulders and marched over to the bar.

Clara waited until she saw the woman take Stephanie's order. She couldn't hear what her cousin was saying, but apparently she'd caught the bartender's attention, as the woman paused and said something over her shoulder before filling a glass with more of the tasteless wine.

Satisfied that Stephanie was handling her side of it, Clara headed for the opposite end of the bar, where the young bartender was joking with a couple of male customers. He left them immediately as Clara sat down at the counter.

"What can I get for you, sweetheart?"

He leered at her, and she had to fight the temptation to tell him she was not his sweetheart and to get lost. Instead, she ordered the chardonnay and waited for him to bring it back to her. She had mixed feelings when he rested his elbow on the counter and gave her another sickly grin.

He shook his head when she offered him her credit card. "It's on the house. We like to take care of our new customers."

I bet, she thought, managing to give him a smile. "Thanks!" She lifted the glass and took a sip, trying not to make a face .

"So, what brings you in here? I haven't seen you around before. On vacation?"

She ignored the questions and gave him her sweetest smile. "This is a real nice bowling alley."

"Yeah." He glanced around. "We do all right. So, where're you from?"

"New York." It was only half a lie, and she felt justified in telling it.

"No kidding." The bartender held out his hand. "I'm Jason, and I'm real happy to meet another New Yorker."

She should have known from the accent. Bracing herself, she returned his strong handshake. "Clara. I heard someone was murdered out there in the parking lot the other night." Her shudder was deliberately exaggerated. "Not something I expected to hear in a town like this."

Jason nodded, his face sober. "Not good for business, I can tell you."

"Did you know him?" She put down her glass. "The victim, I mean."

"Nope. He was from out of town. Portland, I think." Jason reluctantly left her to fill another customer's order.

While she waited, Clara glanced down the counter. Stephanie sat at the far end of the bar with an unhappy look on her face. The bartender was farther up the counter, chatting and laughing with two young men. Apparently her cousin had struck out with the questions. So now it was up to her.

She kept an eye on Jason and smiled at him when he glanced her way. As she'd hoped, he took that as an invitation and strolled back to lean on the counter in front of her. "So, how long are you in town?"

"Awhile." She looked deep into his eyes. "That's if there aren't any more murders going on around here."

Jason grinned. "I can promise you, you're safe here. The cops have got the guy who did it."

"Really?" She opened her eyes wide.

"Yeah. He owns the hardware store on Main Street. He was in here having a couple of beers that night. Didn't look like the kind of guy who goes around beating up people. Just goes to show, you never know who you're dealing with these days."

Clara gasped. "That must have been awful, finding out one of your customers had been killed right on your doorstep."

Jason shrugged. "Yeah, well, like I said, I didn't know the dead guy. Never saw him before that night. Though one of my regulars recognized him the minute his pic came up on TV."

Clara hid her leap of excitement by gulping down a mouthful of wine. She swallowed too fast and spent the next few seconds coughing and spluttering to clear her throat. Out of the corner of her eye she saw Stephanie staring at her from the other end of the bar and prayed her cousin would stay put just a little longer.

"That must have been a shock for him," she said, her voice sounding raw and croaky. "Or is it a *her*?"

"I promise you, Buzz is definitely a *him*." Jason tipped his head on one side. "You okay?"

Eyes watering, she nodded. "He's one of your regular customers?"

"He's here most nights, yeah."

"Is he here tonight?"

Jason looked around. "Nope. Can't see him anywhere."

"He was here the night of the murder?"

"Yeah, I think so."

"*Buzz?* That's a weird name. Is he in show business or something?"

Jason laughed. "The only way you'd see Buzz Lamont on TV is if he got arrested." His face changed, as if he'd just realized he'd said too much. "Forget that," he added sharply. "Why all the questions, anyway? You a cop or something?"

Clara managed a light laugh as she slid off the bar stool. "No thanks. I wouldn't want to be a cop for a million dollars."

Jason stared at her, his eyes narrowed in suspicion.

"Gotta go." She flapped her hand at him. "Thanks for

the drink." She turned and fled across the room to the door, still coughing as she barged out into the foyer.

"What happened?" Stephanie sounded out of breath as she charged out of the bar. "I thought you were going to throw up in there."

"So did I." Clara grabbed her arm and dragged her out into the parking lot. She waited until she could speak without croaking before adding, "I found out something."

"Good," Stephanie said, her voice low with disgust. "I'm glad somebody did. That woman behind the bar is a total moron. I asked her if she knew the murder victim and she acted like I'd asked her if she'd slept with him. She went all tight-lipped and told me she didn't waste her time gossiping about stuff that had nothing to do with her. *Sheez!* Everyone around me went all silent too, like they were afraid I'd arrest them or something. Honestly—"

"Steffie."

She paused, her face looking white in the neon lights of the parking lot. "What?"

"Don't you want to know what I found out?"

"Oh! Of course I do." She glanced around as if checking to see if anyone else was listening. "Okay, go on. Tell me. What did you hear?"

Clara recounted her conversation with the bartender.

Stephanie looked disappointed when she'd finished. "I don't see how that helps, just because the guy recognized the murder victim."

"Doesn't it seem odd to you that he didn't call the

police to identify the victim? They were asking all over town if anyone knew him."

Stephanie's face lit up. "Oh, I get it. He kept quiet because he could be the guy the murder victim came here to meet."

"Right." Clara started heading toward her car. "I think we need to have a word with this Buzz Lamont."

Stephanie trotted after her. "Isn't that going to be dangerous? What if he's the killer?"

"We'll have to be extra careful where we talk to him. It had better be in broad daylight somewhere where other people are around."

"Did you find out where he lived?"

"I was lucky to get a name. We'll have to find out where he lives on our own." She paused at her car and looked across the parking lot to where a row of sycamores lined the railings. Beyond them could be heard the dull popping of rifles from the shooting range. The sound seemed to add to the sinister atmosphere and she shivered, in spite of the warm, humid air surrounding them. "Right now all I want to do is get out of this place and go home."

A car pulled in and parked in the far corner, and Stephanie turned to look at it. "Me, too. It gives me the creeps, knowing someone was probably murdered just a few feet away."

Clara couldn't have agreed more. "Then let's go home."

Stephanie laid a hand on her arm. "Clara, before we go any further, are you absolutely sure Rick had nothing to do with that man? I mean, Dan wouldn't keep him down at the station unless he had good reason, don't you think?"

Fighting down her own doubts, Clara said firmly, "I saw the fight. In a vision. I know it wasn't Rick."

Stephanie's eyebrows shot up. "Then you saw who did it?"

"I wish I had. I couldn't make out the faces." Clara smiled at her. "Don't worry, Steffie. I wouldn't be doing all this if I didn't feel certain that Rick is innocent."

That seemed to satisfy her cousin and she dropped her hand. "What am I going to tell George? He's bound to ask me how the bowling went."

"Tell him we had dinner and we got to talking and before we knew it the time had flown by and it was too late to bowl."

Stephanie nodded. "I'll tell him you had dinner. He'll know I wouldn't eat all that much after already eating dinner at home."

"Sounds good." Clara opened the car door. "I'll see you tomorrow."

"Are we going to tell Molly about this?"

Clara paused and looked back at her. "Do you really want to?"

"I hate keeping secrets from her. Besides, it'll be hard hiding everything we're doing from her, and we could really use her help."

Clara gave in. "I guess you're right."

"Good!" Stephanie waved, and ran over to her own car, a couple of slots away.

Clara waited until she saw her cousin pull out of the parking lot before following her onto the road. She could hardly blame Stephanie for having doubts. Dan had to have some kind of evidence to hold Rick at the station. She just wished she knew what it was.

If it hadn't been for the vision, she might have doubted him, too. Even now, she found it hard to trust the Sense. Was the vision real, or was it just wishful thinking on her part? Was she so eager to defend Rick Sanders, she'd conjured up the image in her mind? If only she could be sure.

Watching the rear lights of Stephanie's car ahead of her, she wrestled with her misgivings as they swept along the coast road. She could see the faint outline of the mountains against the star-studded sky, and the rocky coastline sweeping around the bay.

Tatters would be waiting for her when she got home. Maybe she'd take him for a walk before going to bed. She wondered if the dog missed Rick. She'd miss him herself if he ended up in jail. Horrified at the thought, she dragged her attention back to the road.

The Rick she knew was not a killer. She believed that with all her heart. Whatever had happened that night at the bowling alley had nothing to do with him. He was simply in the wrong place at the wrong time. Whether or not the vision was real, she'd vowed to do everything in her power to find out the truth and nothing was going to stop her.

6

Jessie was already in bed when Clara arrived home. Tatters had obviously been waiting for her. Freed from the formidable gaze that had held him in check all evening, he threw himself at Clara the minute she stepped through the door.

With her back against the wall, Clara tried to avoid the wet tongue lashing at her face. *"Sit!"* she hissed, and when that didn't work, she raised her voice. "I said, *sit!*"

Jessie's voice called out from down the hallway. "Tatters! Don't make me come out there!"

Tatters whined and lowered his haunches to the floor.

Shaking her head, Clara scratched his neck then headed for the kitchen, the dog padding close on her heels.

Mindful of disturbing her mother any further, Clara switched on the small TV on the counter and turned down the volume. Opening the fridge door, she took out a can of soda and carried it to the table. Tatters watched her, his tail swishing back and forth in expectation. "I don't have anything to eat," she told him, "so you can quit the pathetic eyeballing."

Tatters stuck his tongue out the corner of his mouth and started panting.

Clara ignored him as Tom Wright's voice caught her attention. The news anchor looked earnestly into the camera as he announced, "Rick Sanders, the owner of Parson's Hardware on Main Street, continues to be held for questioning in the murder of Frank Tomeski, the Portland construction worker murdered in the parking lot of the Harbor Bowling Alley. We are awaiting further developments and will keep you informed. Stay tuned for . . ."

Clara stared at the TV, trying to drown out the voices whispering urgently in her head. They were trying to tell her something. Possibly something she didn't want to know. How she hated having to listen to them. If they could ease the awful ache of worry in her chest, however, she had no choice but to hear what they had to say.

She closed her eyes and made herself relax, concentrating on the whispering words.

The voices kept fading in and out, like gentle waves washing ashore. She couldn't make out what they were saying. She heard Tatters' soft whine and opened her eyes, laying a hand on his head to reassure him. The walls of the kitchen seemed to fade and dissolve, lost in a white fog that swirled around her.

She quickly closed her eyes again and immediately saw the ocean, the waves rushing in to cover the sand. A sign came into view, swinging in the wind. She could see letters on it but couldn't make them out. *W-i-n . . . f-t . . . m . . . e-l . . .*

Tatters whined again, louder this time. The vision vanished, and when she opened her eyes, the walls were back in focus.

She got up and hurried over to the counter. In the top drawer she found a notebook and pen and quickly scribbled as much of the letters as she could remember. *W-i-n-f-t-m-e-l.*

She stared at them for several long moments, trying to figure out what they meant. When nothing came to her, she gave up. Looking down at a hopeful Tatters, she muttered, "I might as well take you for a walk before I go to bed."

The words were hardly out of her mouth before the big dog leapt through the kitchen door and bounded out into the hallway.

Following him, Clara picked up his leash from the hall table and fastened the clip to his collar. One hand on the doorknob, she bent down to speak in his ear, just on the chance he really could understand what she said. "Any future walks at night will depend entirely on how you behave tonight. Do I make myself clear?"

Tatters licked her nose.

Taking that for agreement, Clara opened the door. Tatters dashed out onto the step, dragging her after him.

It took three more lectures before she finally got him to walk at a pace she could keep up with, by which time she'd circled the block twice and figured that was enough for the first night.

In the morning, she decided, she'd take him for a run on the beach before she went to work. He'd have to make that do until she got home again.

Returning home, she showed him his bed in the utility room. Leaving him there with the scruffy ball, she made another mental note to buy him a couple of decent toys. She'd hardly closed the door of her bedroom when she heard him whining.

Hoping he'd settle down quickly, she ignored the mournful sound and got ready for bed. She had just climbed under the covers when Tatters let out a howl of protest.

She was opening her bedroom door when she heard her mother's voice.

"That dog shuts up *now*, or he's gone in the morning."

Clara sighed, and called out, "I'll take care of it."

Opening the door of the utility room, she stood in the doorway, barring Tatters' escape. Hands on her hips, she looked him in the eye. "This is *not* acceptable behavior. If you want to stay here, you will have to abide by the rules. You sleep in *here*." She pointed at the bed. "I don't want to hear another sound. Is that clear?"

Tatters whined.

Clara shut the door and had barely gone a few steps when the dog howled again.

Jessie's outraged roar echoed down the hallway.

Wincing, Clara opened the door again. The dog's tongue was hanging out of the corner of his mouth in the familiar grin.

Clara leaned forward and gripped his collar. "I'm too tired to deal with you now, so just for tonight, you sleep with me. Just for tonight, you understand?" Tatters wagged his tail.

Sighing, Clara led him into her bedroom and closed the door. Knowing she was going to regret her weakness, she watched Tatters leap onto the bed and settle himself down on her pillow. At the first opportunity, she promised herself, she'd have a talk with him. Right now, however, she was exhausted and just wanted to crawl into bed and forget about everything—the murder, Rick's involvement, the strange letters in the vision, the problems with the dog—everything. At least until morning.

She spent most of the night wrestling with the dog for space on the pillow before falling into a fitful sleep. Waking up again with a start, she saw sunlight sparkling between the slats of the blinds at her window. She could hear an odd sound, like the distant rumble of a freight train. It took her a moment or two to realize it was Tatters' snoring that had disturbed her sleep.

Which was just as well, as a quick glance at the clock confirmed that she'd overslept. Jessie must have already left for work. Clara hoped her mother hadn't checked the utility room and realized that Tatters was sharing her daughter's bed. She'd have plenty to say about that if she had.

After swallowing a couple of slices of toast and a cup of coffee, Clara took Tatters for a quick walk around the block. "I'll take you to the beach when I get home from work," she promised him, trying to ignore the pleading look in his eyes when she closed the bedroom door on him.

Stephanie was waiting for her when she walked into the Raven's Nest a few minutes later. "We have to talk," her cousin said as Clara stuffed her purse under the counter. Without waiting for an answer, she marched off down the aisle, leaving Clara to follow.

Molly was talking to a customer at the counter and gave her a quick wave as she passed. Clara wondered if Stephanie had already asked for her help with their efforts to clear Rick's name. In light of the latest news that they were still holding Rick at the police station, however, Clara wasn't sure if Stephanie was still willing to go ahead with it.

She entered the Nook to find her cousin pouring out two mugs of coffee. Stephanie handed her one of the mugs and sat down on the couch. "Have you heard any more news?"

Clara sank onto the nearest armchair. "Not since last night."

"So what do you think?"

Clara leaned back, cradling the mug in her hands. "I just wish I could talk to Rick and get his side of the story. So far all we've heard is Dan's side of it."

"Carson Dexter seems to think the case is about to be solved."

"He's certainly not helping matters," Clara said, letting a note of bitterness creep into her voice. "Anyone listening to him would think that Rick has already been tried and convicted. What happened to the law that says that every person must be presumed innocent until proven guilty?"

"It still stands, the last I heard."

"Well, listening to our honorable mayor, you'd never know it even existed."

Stephanie heaved a heavy sigh. "So, what are we going to do? Did you find out where this Buzz person lives?"

"Buzz Lamont. Not yet." Clara stared gloomily into her mug. "I don't think we'll get much out of him. If he didn't want to talk to the police, he sure won't talk to us. All we know so far is that he recognized the victim on TV. By the way, the dead guy's name is Frank Tomeski."

"Oh, right! How did you remember that? So do you think he came to Finn's Harbor to meet this Buzz Lamont person?"

"Maybe, though I doubt Mr. Lamont would tell us if he did."

Stephanie sipped her coffee before answering. "I guess you could just ask him, and maybe the Sense will help you tell if he's lying. You've done that plenty of times before. Like the time Old Man Thompson told you he kept a wolf in his house to scare off trespassers. You knew he was lying and climbed through a window of his house to prove it."

Clara gave her a withering look. "I climbed through

the window because you dared me to do it. I got caught and ended up getting grounded for a week. You didn't even get yelled at."

Stephanie shrugged. "I wanted to know if you could really tell when someone's lying."

"Sometimes I can and a lot of times I can't."

She hadn't meant to sound so bitter. Stephanie reached out to pat her arm. "I'm sorry, Clara. I didn't mean to bring up bad memories."

Clara nodded. She'd given her cousin a brief version of what had happened in New York, but had told no one the whole story. The truth was, she wasn't ready to talk about it. Or even think about it. Maybe she never would be ready. "Well, I guess it won't hurt to give it a shot with Buzz Lamont. If we can find out where he lives." Her memory prodded, she dug in her pants pocket for the note she'd scribbled the night before. "Speaking of which, I had a sort of vision last night."

Stephanie sat up, her eyes bright with expectation. "Another one? What was it?"

"Nothing much. Just a sign swinging in the wind. Some of the letters were too faded to read, but here's what I remember of it." Handing the note to her cousin, she added, "See if this means anything to you."

Stephanie studied the note. Frowning, she shook her head. "It doesn't make sense."

"Try and imagine it with other letters in between."

Stephanie started muttering. "Winfutmel . . . Winningfutmel . . . Windingfutmel . . ."

Molly's voice made them both jump. "What are you doing?"

Stephanie quickly folded the note and shoved it in the pocket of her blue smock. "Just playing word games. Did Mrs. Riley buy anything?"

"No, but she ordered a couple of books." Molly wandered over to the counter and picked up the coffeepot. "It's quiet out there today."

Stephanie questioned with her eyes, a message Clara instantly understood. Her cousin wanted to know if it was okay to tell Molly about their investigation. She gave her a quick nod of approval. Stephanie answered with a finger jabbed in her direction.

Taking that to mean she was to open the conversation, Clara said lightly, "I guess you heard the latest news about Rick?"

Molly nodded as she walked over to the couch. "I still can't believe it. He seems such a nice guy." She shot a wary glance at Clara. "You must be really upset about all this."

"I'm upset at people jumping to the conclusion he's guilty," Clara said, her voice sharp with annoyance. Catching her cousin's quick frown, she added more calmly, "Stephanie and I plan to do something about that."

Molly looked at Stephanie, who beamed at her. "We thought you might like to help, too."

A multitude of expressions crossed Molly's face. It was obvious she was struggling between her conviction of Rick's guilt and her loyalty to her friends.

Clara decided to help her out. "He didn't do it," she said firmly. "We are quite sure of that."

"I really want to believe you, but the cops say—"

"Never mind what they say," Stephanie said, beating Clara to the punch. "It's what *we* believe that matters. You can't have forgotten that you were in the same boat last year, Molly. Everyone thought you were guilty until we found the real murderer."

Molly's face turned pink. "Of course I haven't forgotten. I owe you guys a lot. It's just that . . . well, the mayor sounded so convinced . . ."

Clara made a guttural sound in her throat. "Don't get me started on that. He's just looking for a boost to his political career. Rick didn't kill that man, and we're going to prove it. Are you in or not?"

Molly stared at her for a long moment, then shrugged. "What do you want me to do?"

Both cousins let out a sigh of relief.

"See if you can make sense of these letters," Stephanie said, handing Molly the note.

Molly studied it, her brows drawn together as she concentrated. "What is it?"

"I saw it on a sign somewhere," Clara said quickly, before Stephanie could answer. "Some of the letters are missing. We were wondering if you recognized it."

Molly shook her head and handed the note back to Stephanie. "Sorry. It doesn't mean anything to me."

"Oh, well, we tried." Stephanie tilted her head to one

side as the jingle of the front doorbell interrupted her. "Sounds like a customer."

Molly put down her mug and jumped up. "I'll go." She actually looked relieved as she sped out of the Nook, and Clara made a face at her cousin. "I don't think she's going to help that much."

Stephanie got up from the couch and handed Clara the note. "Give her a chance. She'll come around. I'd better get going. My mother will be waiting for me to pick up the kids."

Clara followed her up the aisle to the front of the shop, her nerves tightening when she saw Molly at the counter talking to Roberta Prince. That was all she needed.

Roberta seemed agitated, talking very fast and loud, while Molly just stood there nodding her head. Stephanie hurried forward, saying, "Can I help you?"

No one can help that woman, Clara thought, then felt guilty for being uncharitable. She hung back, ready to step in if Stephanie needed her.

"I just can't believe it!" Roberta flung a carefully manicured hand at Stephanie in a dramatic gesture that would have gone over well on the stage. "What the hell was he thinking?"

Stephanie looked at Molly for help and received a shrug in answer. "Who are we talking about?"

"Rick, of course!" Roberta tugged at the colorful silk scarf that decorated her white shirt. "How could he have bludgeoned a man to death? I know he has a bit of a temper, but I never thought he would go this far."

Clara closed her eyes, willing herself to stay silent.

To her surprise, she heard Molly say firmly, "Rick hasn't actually been charged with murder. He's just being questioned, that's all."

"Yeah," Stephanie added, "that doesn't prove a thing. All it means is that so far he's the only one with any connection to the victim."

Roberta scowled at her. "The body was found in Rick's truck, and the murder weapon came from his store. What more do you need to be convinced he's guilty?"

Clara could hold it in no longer. "A whole lot more. I should think you, of all people, would have some faith in him, considering you've been chasing after him all these months."

"Clara—" Stephanie began, but Roberta silenced her with a swift movement of her hand.

Tossing her head, she advanced on Clara. "Trust me, darling, I have never, *ever* needed to chase after anybody. I'm usually the one running away. Rick and I have a special relationship, and until now I was under the impression that he was a decent, law-abiding citizen. Now that the police have arrested him for murder, I'll have to reevaluate our friendship. If I were you, I'd do the same."

"Rick hasn't been arrested." The soft voice spoke from the doorway, startling them all. No one had noticed the sound of the doorbell, and all heads turned to stare at the newcomer.

John Halloran stood in the doorway, smirking in his delight at causing a disturbance.

Stephanie was the first one to recover. She rushed forward, rudely shoving Roberta aside. "Has something happened? What have you heard?"

Obviously enjoying all the attention, John stepped forward and let the door close behind him. "I know," he said, in a slow, deliberate tone, "because Rick is at this very minute across the street in the shop."

Four voices gasped, then all spoke at once.

"When did they let him go?'

"What happened?'

"Thank heavens!"

"Is he okay?" Clara grabbed John's arm. "He's all right, isn't he?"

John's eyes gleamed behind his glasses. "Why don't you go see for yourself?"

Roberta fluffed her blonde hair back from her face. "Well, *I'm* going to wait for more news before I go see him." She stalked over to the door. "If I were you, Clara, I'd think twice about associating with a murder suspect."

Clara ignored her and turned to Stephanie. Before she could say anything, Stephanie laid a hand on her arm.

"Go ahead. I'll hang on here until you get back."

Clara gave her a quick, grateful hug, then dashed out the door. Passing Roberta on the curb, she ran across the street to the hardware store.

Inside the shop, she paused for a moment or two for her eyes to adjust to the contrast from the dazzling sunlight outside. She could see Rick on his knees at the far end of the store, unpacking a large box of electric fans.

She couldn't see his expression, and uncertain of his mood, she approached him warily. He looked up as she reached him and, to her relief, gave her a wide smile.

Getting to his feet, he said lazily, "Not afraid to visit the felon, then?"

She uttered a snort of disgust. "Idiots. What on earth was Dan thinking, hauling you off to the station like that?"

Rick shrugged. "Can't say I blame him. Things have been going from bad to worse. Luckily I have a good lawyer."

"So you're in the clear?"

He rubbed a hand across his forehead. "Not exactly. The cops didn't have enough evidence to hold me, so Dan let me go with a warning not to leave town."

Clara winced. "Ouch. So what are you going to do now?"

"Wait, I guess. And pray a lot."

"I don't blame you." She considered telling him that she and Stephanie were trying to find out who did kill Frank Tomeski, but decided that it was better not to say anything until they had something useful to offer him.

"So, how is Tatters doing?" Rick picked up the empty box and headed for the counter.

Following him, Clara said lightly, "He's doing fine. I think he misses you, though."

Rick swung around to look at her. "Really? I thought he hated me. I was always yelling at him."

She smiled. "Dogs don't hate you for yelling at them. They are the most forgiving of all creatures. I've been doing some yelling myself, but Tatters and I are best buddies."

"Has he been giving you a hard time?"

Thinking about her sleepless night, she nevertheless shook her head. "He's settling down very well. You should see him with my mother. He sleeps at her feet while she's watching TV."

Rick grinned. "That I've got to see."

"Then why don't you come over for dinner some night and witness it for yourself."

The words were out before she realized what she was saying. She waited nervously for his answer, wondering if she'd stepped over the line. To her relief, he replied with a laugh. "Maybe I will . . . sometime."

Deciding it was time to change the subject, she picked up a hammer from the display on his counter. "Is this like the one that was used in the murder?"

His expression changed instantly, and again she could have bitten her tongue for saying the wrong thing. What was it about Rick Sanders that turned her mind to complete mush when she was around him?

"Yes." He took it from her. "I wish now I'd set up security cameras in the store. I might have seen who stole the murder weapon. I thought about it when I took over the business, but this is such a small town and everybody knows everybody. Putting up cameras to spy on my customers felt like I didn't trust them or something. It just didn't seem right."

"We do get a lot of tourists in the summer."

"True." He put the hammer back in the display. "But not many who shop in a hardware store."

"I guess not." Seeing the strain in his face unsettled her. "Well, it's good to see you back here. We were all worried about you."

"I was pretty worried myself." He leaned against the counter and crossed his arms. "Especially when the cops found out I'd served Tomeski here in the store the day he died. They were so sure I'd lied about that to cover up the fact that I knew him. Jarvis, my lawyer, was able to convince Dan that I was too busy that day to remember him. At least enough for him to let me go for now."

"So if the murderer stole the hammer from you, both he and the victim have been here in the store."

"I guess so." Rick unfolded his arms and straightened up a pile of pamphlets on the counter. "Like I said, not many tourists come in here. It could have been one of the locals."

"Well, I'm sure Dan will find out who killed Frank Tomeski soon, and then you'll be off the hook."

"I sure hope you're right." His worried frown made her ache with sympathy for him. "It's not much fun being suspected of murder. I can feel everyone staring at me, wondering if I did it."

"I'm sure you're imagining things. Anyone who knows you has to know you couldn't possibly have killed that man."

He gave her a wry smile. "Roberta Prince thinks I did it."

"No, she doesn't." Clara started for the door. "She's just afraid it will ruin her image if she's seen in your company. That's all she cares about."

"Well, if it keeps her from showing up at my door every five minutes, I'd say that's a good thing."

Clara paused at the door and looked back at him. "Don't let this get to you. Your friends believe in you and we'll stand by you. Hang in there."

He raised his hand in farewell. "Thanks, Clara. That means a lot."

Warmed by his smile, she left the shop and crossed the street to the bookstore. Somehow she would have to find out who had killed Frank Tomeski and clear Rick's name. The sooner the better. "Come on, Sense," she muttered as she reached the door of the Raven's Nest. "Where are you when I need you?"

As if in answer a voice whispered in her ear. *Windrift.*

7

Clara didn't have a chance to talk to Stephanie when she returned to the bookstore. Her cousin rushed past her the moment she opened the door. "Can't stop. Mom's waiting for me. Talk to you later!" With a wave of her hand she was gone, darting to and fro down the crowded sidewalk.

Molly was busy serving a customer, and Clara walked over to the counter and sat down at the computer. With any luck there'd be no more customers to disturb her for a while. It took only a minute to look up the white pages directory. There were four Lamonts listed. Clara scribbled down the numbers on a pad and tucked the note in her pocket.

The doorbell jangled, announcing another customer. Looking up, Clara saw Roberta Prince heading for the counter. Molly had disappeared down one of the aisles. There was no way of escaping another charming conversation with the woman.

Bracing herself, Clara waited for Roberta to speak first. She didn't have to wait long. Roberta paused in front of the counter, leaned her hands on the surface and said, "Tell me everything."

Pretending she had no idea what that meant, Clara raised her eyebrows. "I beg your pardon?"

Roberta waved an impatient hand at the window. "Rick, of course. Tell me what happened."

"Why don't you ask him yourself?"

"I don't want to disturb him. I'm sure he's got enough to worry about right now without having everyone on the street asking him questions." Roberta straightened, drawing the back of her hand across her forehead. "Besides, I have a beastly headache. I think I need to lie down."

Clara seized the opportunity to change the subject. "So, how's the new assistant coming along?"

"Totally useless, of course." Roberta tossed her head in disgust. "I've had to be behind her every step of the way. Unbelievable. It's impossible to find anyone with any intelligence in this town."

Clara nodded in sympathy, though it was evident to her that Roberta's problem with assistants was in the way she treated them, rather than any flaws in their performance. So far, none that she had hired had stayed longer than a month or so. "Maybe she just needs more time,"

Clara said, feeling sorry for the timid young woman she'd met only briefly in the stationer's.

Roberta uttered a mirthless laugh. "It will take more than time to make a decent assistant out of that one." She glanced at the door. "I heard that Rick was planning on hiring an assistant to help out John. I guess he'll have to put that on hold now."

Clara kept her expression blank. "Why's that?"

"Well, with everything going on over there." Roberta frowned. "I wonder what he'll do with the business if he goes to jail. Sell it, I suppose. John won't be able to run it for him."

"What makes you think he's going to jail?"

Roberta gave her a sharp look. "The last I heard, he was the main suspect in a murder."

"Obviously there's some doubt about that, or he'd be in custody."

Roberta sniffed. "You are entirely too trusting, Clara. When you've been around as many men as I have, you'll learn that none of them can be trusted. No matter how decent or honest they may appear. Men are beasts. That will never change."

Clara held her breath for a long moment before letting it out. Roberta's words had hit home, and she wasn't about to let the woman know that part of her agreed wholeheartedly. She was struggling with her own insecurities, but she had to believe that not all men were deceitful and insincere. There had to be some good ones out there.

To her relief, Roberta wandered off down an aisle, leaving her alone at the counter. She waited a moment or two to make sure no one else was heading toward her, then pulled the note from her pocket. Opening up her cell phone, she dialed the first number on the list.

The elderly female voice that answered assured her that no one named Buzz lived there. "I live alone," the woman added. "I have never heard of Buzz Lamont. I'm sure I would have remembered if I had."

Clara thanked her and dialed the second number. It was a male voice this time—a recorded message that informed her she had reached Philip Lamont, who was not at home. Clara dialed again, wondering if Buzz was Philip Lamont's nickname.

A younger voice answered this time, and the woman sounded impatient. Once more Clara asked for Buzz Lamont and got a short answer in response. "Who's this?"

Pulse quickening, Clara thought fast. "I'm doing a survey on local politics and I would like to ask Mr. Lamont for his opinion."

After a slight hesitation, the woman spoke again. "Buzz is at work. He won't be home until early evening. I don't think he could help you, anyway. He's not too interested in politics."

"Ah, but this survey could actually be beneficial to him. What kind of work does he do?"

Again the pause. Longer this time. Clara held her breath.

"He's a gardener. He works for Belgrave Landscaping."

Clara smiled. "Perfect. Perhaps I can catch him at work."

Now the woman sounded worried. "I don't think—"

"Don't worry, I won't be a pest or anything. Thank you so much for your time." Clara snapped her phone shut, well pleased with herself.

"What are you grinning about?"

Startled, Clara raised her chin and found Molly smiling at her. "I'll tell you later," she said, wary of mentioning anything about the investigation while Roberta Prince was in the store. "By the way, have you ever heard of the name *Windrift*? Does it mean anything to you?"

Molly frowned. "It sounds familiar, though I don't know why. Let me think about it. It might come to me."

"Okay. Let me know if you remember where you heard it."

Molly nodded, then turned as the doorbell jingled again. A young girl darted into the store, anxiously looking around. "I lost my copy of *Huckleberry Finn* and I can't find it anywhere. I'm supposed to read it this summer. The library just checked out their last copy. Do you still have the required reading list for high school?"

"We keep a supply of required reading books on these shelves," Molly said, leading the anxious girl down an aisle. "Let's see if we have it there."

Clara glanced at the clock. It was too soon to call Stephanie to tell her she'd found out where Buzz Lamont worked. It would have to wait until later that afternoon. She shoved the note in her pocket, and her fingers collided with another piece of paper. Drawing it out, she glanced at it, prepared to throw it away. The letters scribbled on the paper stopped her. It was the note she'd made of the letters in her vision. *W-i-n-f-t-m-e-l.*

She stared at them, excitement building as she mentally added letters. *Windrift.* That had to be it. But what was the rest? She stared at the note some more, and then it dawned on her. *Windrift Motel.* Of course. Now she remembered seeing the sign swinging in the sea breeze. It was a motel on the coast road. She caught her breath, hearing her mother's words again. *Apparently he was here on vacation and was staying at one of those dreadful motels on the coast road.*

Frank Tomeski had been staying at the Windrift Motel. That's what the Sense had been trying to tell her. Maybe if she talked to the motel manager, she might find out something useful. Now she could hardly wait to tell her cousin what she'd learned.

It was much later that afternoon before Clara found herself alone in the Raven's Nest. Molly had left for the day, and the usual late-afternoon lull had emptied out the store. Clara speed-dialed Stephanie's number and prayed she'd answer.

Her cousin sounded frazzled as usual. "I've just fished Michael out of the washing machine. Olivia was about to give him a ride. She'd told him it was a time machine that would send him to Disney World. She's eight years old for heaven's sake! When is she ever going to join the real world?"

Clara grinned. "She sounds just like you when you were her age."

"I was *never* that irrational. She must take after George's side of the family. His grandfather was a bomber pilot in World War Two. From what I've heard, he was totally insane."

"Well, I'm sure Olivia is just a normal little girl with a wild streak, that's all. At least no one got hurt."

"*This* time," Stephanie muttered. "Heaven knows what might happen if I didn't keep a strict eye on her. And Michael is so gullible. I don't know how he's going to get along in first grade this fall. He believes everything he's told."

"You worry far too much. Remember how our parents used to worry about us? They were always telling us about all the bad things that could happen to us if we didn't mend our ways."

Stephanie's sigh drifted clearly down the line. "That's what worries me. When I remember some of the things we did when we were kids, I shudder to think what my kids could get into. The world is a very different place now."

Clara was inclined to agree. Hoping to take her cousin's mind off her worries, she said quickly, "I deciphered the words on that note I gave you this morning."

Stephanie's tone changed at once. "You did? What is it? Tell me!"

"It's the Windrift Motel. Which I believe just happens

to be the motel where Frank Tomeski was staying. I thought we might go there and talk to the manager. Maybe he knows something that could help us figure out what really happened."

"Good idea. When do you want to go?"

"How about tomorrow morning? Before I start my shift? Molly could watch things for a while on her own, right?"

"I suppose so. I'll call her and let her know."

"There's something else. I found out where Buzz Lamont works. I thought we could talk to him as well."

Stephanie's voice was full of doubt. "Are you sure that's wise? What if he *is* the killer? He could figure we know too much and attack us or something."

"That's why we're going to talk to him where he works. He can't very well do anything violent there."

"So where does he work?"

"He's a gardener with Belgrave Landscaping."

Her cousin's voice grew quieter. "That doesn't sound very safe. What if he's alone in a big garden somewhere with pruning shears or something?" Her voice rose a notch or two. "I don't like it at all. Maybe we should just tell the police what we know and let Dan question him."

"Maybe Dan's already questioned him. In any case, it's unlikely Mr. Lamont would admit to anything."

"So why would he tell us anything important, then?"

"He wouldn't. But we have something Dan doesn't."

"What's that?"

Clara puffed out her breath. "The Quinn Sense."

"Oh, right." Stephanie paused, then added, "But you said it's not reliable."

"It's not, but it's the only shot we've got."

There was an even longer pause before her cousin asked, "So, you think Buzz Lamont killed Tamaski . . . or whatever his name is?"

"Tomeski." Clara took a moment to steady her voice. "I think it's possible. We won't know unless we talk to him."

"All right. We'd better get started early, then."

"Nine or so? I'll meet you here at the bookstore."

"Tomorrow's Saturday. Let's just hope we're not too busy."

"Molly can handle it, and we'll be back before the coffee crowd comes in."

"I hope so. What did Rick have to say this morning?"

Clara repeated as much of the conversation as she could remember, and hung up. To keep her mind off things she busied herself restocking and tidying shelves in between customers until it was time to close up the shop.

The spicy aroma of cooking hung in the sultry evening air as she passed by the Pizza Parlor. The tables were crowded as usual, and she could see Tony Manetas, the owner, standing over a couple of young tourists, waving his pudgy hands in the air as he delivered one of his many stories of his long-lost youth.

Her mother had probably listened to a few of those stories herself, Clara thought as she made her way down the hill to the parking lot. Jessie was certain Tony was infatuated with her, and went to great pains to perpetuate the situation at every opportunity.

Thinking of her mother quickened Clara's step. She had almost forgotten about Tatters, and hoped the dog was still under her mother's control

She arrived home shortly after to find Tatters shut in the utility room, loudly protesting. A note lay on the table from Jessie, explaining that she'd had an invitation she couldn't refuse. Clara wondered if her mother had been in the Pizza Parlor when she'd passed by. Jessie was clearly doing her best to move on after the death of her husband.

Not that Clara could blame her. Jessie was still an attractive woman and looked years younger than her age. Still, she'd hoped her mother would find someone a little more civilized than the loud and somewhat crude Tony Manetas. Her father was a tough act to follow, and she would have thought Jessie would be a little more discriminating in her choice of companions.

Frowning, she opened the door of the utility room and was immediately flattened against the wall by massive paws on her stomach. Gasping for air, she managed to shove the enthusiastic Tatters to the floor and wagged a stern finger at him. *"Sit!"*

He lowered his haunches halfway, then straightened again. Looking up at her, he uttered a soft whine.

"Did she even feed you before she left?" Clara looked in the utility room and saw only a bowl of water. Sighing, she picked it up and carried it to the kitchen, followed by the big dog hot on her heels. After filling Tatters' bowl with his dog food, she made herself a salad and sat down to watch TV.

Jessie still hadn't arrived home when the news came on, and Clara was about to turn off the TV when the announcer introduced Mayor Carson Dexter. She paused long enough to hear the mayor loudly complaining about the release of the suspect in what had been dubbed "the bowling alley murder."

"There is something wrong with our justice system," the mayor declared, "if the authorities are unable to keep a murder suspect under lock and key until enough evidence has been found to convict him. I can only hope that our loved ones are not in danger with a killer loose on the streets of Finn's Harbor."

Clara rolled her eyes and switched off the TV. If she were Rick, she thought as she marched down the hallway to her room, she'd sue the mayor for defamation of character. Still fuming, she changed into sweats and sneakers and picked up Tatters' leash. "Come on, boy. Let's go let off some steam."

Tatters beat her to the front door and pranced around until she opened it. The second there was a few inches of space, he was through it and bounding down the driveway in the dark. Clara yelled out to him as she closed the front door, then froze when she heard the awful sound of screeching brakes.

No! Not Tatters! She spun around, her heart starting to beat again when she saw the big dog leaping up on the driver's side of a red pickup.

A familiar voice called out to her, making her heart beat even faster.

"Rick?" She ran over to the pickup and grabbed Tatters' collar. Snapping on the leash, she looked up into Rick's face. She couldn't tell anything from his expression; his features were too shadowed in the dim light of the streetlamp.

"Rick . . . gosh, I'm so sorry. I should have had his leash on before I opened the door. I was thinking about something else and . . ." To her intense embarrassment, her voice broke, and she quickly cleared her throat.

"Hey, it's okay." Rick opened the door and climbed out, much to the delight of Tatters, who leapt up at him in an attempt to lick his face. Rick hugged the dog, his gaze still fixed on Clara's face. "He's done this to me plenty of times. I told you he was tough to handle."

Clara gave him a wobbly smile. "If anything happened to him, I'd never forgive myself. I promise I'll take better care of him from now on. I just wasn't thinking. I'm so sorry."

"I told you, it's okay." Rick pushed the dog down and moved closer to her. "Is everything all right? I mean, apart from this miserable hound's suicidal behavior?"

"Yes . . . no . . . it's just . . ." She swallowed, aware she was behaving like a complete idiot. With any luck, Rick hadn't seen the interview with the mayor, and she wasn't about to tell him the nasty things Carson Dexter was saying about him or how deeply they seemed to affect her "Call it a bad day," she finished, rather lamely.

If Rick realized she was being evasive, he gave no sign. He punched his key to lock the pickup, then took the leash from her hand. "I assume you were venturing out on a walk with this beast?"

She laughed. "That was the general idea."

"Then let's go. Between the two of us we should be able to keep him from committing hara-kiri."

Feeling suddenly lighthearted, she set out at his side, with Tatters straining at the leash ahead of them.

"Feel like going to the harbor, or is that too far to walk?" Rick asked as they crossed the street.

"Sounds great." Clara nodded at the dog. "Tatters would love that. I've been promising to take him on the beach, but so far I haven't had time to walk him more than a couple of blocks."

Rick sounded amused when he answered. "Don't worry. He won't know you broke a promise."

He'd be surprised what Tatters understood, Clara thought. Not that she could tell Rick that. "Well, I know he'll enjoy running on the sand without a leash." She glanced at him. "I guess he can run without a leash, right?"

"Any time between eight p.m. and sunrise."

"Oh good. I was hoping it would be okay."

"Did you know that the beach areas in Maine all have different rules about dogs being on the beach?"

"No, I didn't." She quickened her step to keep up with him. "I thought they'd all be the same."

"Nope. Some of them don't allow dogs on there at all in the summer. Some don't allow dogs off the leash, and those that do have different times when it's okay. It can be pretty confusing if you're traveling with a dog."

"I can imagine." She giggled. "I can't imagine traveling with Tatters, though."

"He'd need a trailer all to himself."

They both laughed, and Clara felt a warm sense of contentment. This was nice—two friends enjoying a walk with the dog. She couldn't ask for anything better than that.

By the time they'd reached the harbor, the sea breeze had cooled the night air, a welcome relief from the muggy heat of the day. A few people still strolled along the seafront, but the beach was practically deserted. Moonlight sparkled on the water and cast an eerie glow over the sand. Clara shivered. She'd never been fond of the beach at night, even as a teenager. Stephanie had dragged her to more than one bonfire on the beach, and she'd spent most of the time huddled by the leaping flames, reluctant to leave the safety of the light.

She watched Rick let Tatters off the leash, and the dog dashed off, heading straight for the water's edge. She watched him anxiously as he plunged into the waves. "He won't go too far out, will he?"

Rick laughed. "Watch him."

She could just see the dark shape of the dog's head in the water, his nose in the air as he paddled out for a few yards. Then a wave came in and he turned, riding it like a surfer toward the shore. When he could stand, he walked out of the water, shook himself, then bounded off into the darkness.

Before Clara could voice her concern again, Rick whistled, and a moment later a bark answered him. Staring into the darkness, Clara relaxed as the shaggy dog raced into view and chased in circles all around them until he finally got tired and flopped down on the sand.

"There's only one problem with bringing him down here," Rick said as he seated himself on a rock. "He takes half the beach back with him when he goes home."

Clara groaned. "I hadn't thought of that."

Rick grinned and patted the space next to him. "Here. Take the weight off your feet for a few minutes. It's a long walk back."

There wasn't a lot of room on the rock for both of them. Clara sat as near to the edge as she could get, but was still a little too close to him for comfort. She was intensely aware of his arm brushing hers, and did her best to ignore the twittery feeling, as Stephanie described it.

Deciding to take refuge in conversation, she asked, "How did you happen to be outside my house tonight?"

"I was going to pay the monster a visit." He nodded at the dog. "I was kind of worried he might be sabotaging your home and you didn't want to tell me."

"He's been quite good, actually." She smiled at Tatters, who seemed content just to lie on the sand with his nose in his paws. "My mother watches him while I'm at work."

"And how's that working out?"

She shrugged. "Okay, I guess. When my mother's annoyed, her voice takes on a tone that would stop a charging bull. I'm pretty sure she can keep Tatters under control. I haven't heard any complaints, anyway."

"I hope you know how much I appreciate you taking him off my hands." Rick looked serious as he gazed out to sea. "I don't know what I would have done with him if . . ."

He let his voice trail off, but Clara knew the end of that sentence. "You're not going to jail," she said firmly. "No matter what the mayor might say."

Rick turned to her. "What's he been saying?"

Clara inwardly cursed. As usual she'd spoken before she'd thought. Figuring that Rick would hear about it sooner or later, she tried to sound unconcerned. "Oh, he was on TV tonight, running off at the mouth as usual. I don't take any notice of him anymore. I doubt anyone does."

"I wish I could believe that." Rick stared at the ocean again. "I haven't had one customer in the store for the past two days. If this keeps up, I'll be out of business before they solve this murder."

"Oh, Rick, I'm so sorry." Impulsively she laid a hand on his arm. "People can be so thickheaded. Maybe you should call and complain about the mayor's comments.

After all, he's condemning you in public without any just cause."

He glanced down at her hand as if surprised to see it there, and feeling self-conscious, she pulled it back.

"I guess he's convinced I did it." Rick shook his head. "I've met him a couple of times at business meetings and he seems like an okay guy. I guess he's worried about the tourist business. I can't say I blame him. People are likely to give us a wide berth until the killer is caught."

"He should be more worried about his false accusations. It's so unfair to you."

She could see the warmth in his eyes when he smiled at her. "You're a good friend, Clara. I wish—"

Whatever he was going to say was lost in the uproar of Tatters' barking. He'd spotted a potential enemy in a black lab that had the audacity to run too close to him. It took their combined efforts to finally catch up with him and put him back on the leash before peace was restored.

Walking back to the house, Clara kept the conversation on a mundane level. She didn't want to ask what Rick had been about to say before he was interrupted. It was safer not to know. Even so, as she waved good-bye to him and watched his taillights disappear down the street, she couldn't help wondering if the rest of that sentence would have been personal in nature and, if so, what her reaction might have been.

She had wishes, too. She wished that she'd never met her former fiancé. She wished that she could trust her heart again. Then again, perhaps it was just as well. She had a feeling that if she ever let herself get too close to Rick Sanders, she'd fall hard, and that, as she well knew, could lead to unbearable heartbreak.

The thought triggered a memory she had fought so long and hard to forget.

It was the night before the wedding, and she'd spent the day rushing around dealing with the last-minute arrangements for the small, private ceremony. She was exhausted, but too excited to sleep. This would be the last night before she was married to Matt—the wonderful man of her dreams and the man she'd loved with all her heart for more than three years.

She had been about to run a bubble bath when the phone had rung. Surprised to hear Kyle, the best man, on the line, she'd asked him why he wasn't at Matt's bachelor party. Kyle had hesitated for so long she'd grown anxious, sensing something was wrong.

Finally he'd told her. Matt had changed his mind. There would be no wedding.

Devastated and confused, she'd demanded to know where Matt was, saying she needed to talk to him. Kyle had told her that Matt had left town that night, and nobody knew where he'd gone. He hadn't even had the guts to tell her himself.

Days later she'd found out that Matt's secretary had left town with him. Realizing that the man she'd loved and thought she knew didn't exist, she'd vowed never to be that vulnerable again. She'd learned her lesson the hard way, and it was one she would never forget.

Much as she liked Rick, it was better to keep things the way they were—a nice, comfortable relationship with no complications.

As she opened the front door, her inner voice spoke loud and clear. *Who are you kidding?*

8

Clara arrived first at the Raven's Nest the next morning. Catching sight of Rick stacking garden tools in a barrel across the street, she waved and received an answering wave back. She opened the front door, frowning at the memory of their conversation the night before.

Rick was worried, and had every right to be. People were inclined to believe whatever they read in the newspaper or saw on the news, and so far, everything seemed to be pointing to his guilt. The mayor's comments definitely weren't helping, and although Rick's lawyer had managed to keep him out of custody so far, she had to wonder for how long. She and Stephanie needed to get down to business, and fast.

Molly arrived just as the coffee had finished perking.

"You must have smelled it," Clara said as Molly joined her in the Reading Nook.

"All the way from the harbor." Molly grinned as she accepted a steaming mug. "What are you doing here so early?"

"I'm meeting Stephanie. We're going to run some errands."

Molly nodded. "Oh, that's right. She called me last night. She said you two had some stuff to take care of this morning. By the way, I remembered where I'd seen *Windrift*. It's a motel on the coast road."

"Thanks. I realized it myself last night." Clara sipped her coffee.

"They mentioned it on the news this morning." Molly wandered over to the couch and sat down. "It's the motel where the murdered guy was staying."

It was obvious Molly was curious, but Clara was still wary of telling her too many details. The less the young woman knew, the better. "Yes," she said, "I thought it might be."

Too bad they didn't mention it before, she thought. It would have saved her some headaches trying to decipher the letters in her vision. Then again, if she hadn't had the vision, she might not have thought about questioning the motel manager.

Drat the Quinn Sense. She'd spent so many years trying to drum it out of her head; now it was even more elusive than ever.

"So, how's the detective work going?"

Faced with the direct question, Clara found it difficult to be evasive. She'd agreed with Stephanie that Molly should be included in their investigation, or at least informed. Still, she would rather her cousin was there when Molly learned of their plans.

Fortunately, Stephanie appeared before Clara had to answer. Her cousin rushed into the Nook, breathless and apologetic. "George had to leave early this morning, and it took forever to get the kids ready to go to their grandma's house." She wiped her brow with the back of her hand. "Ethan wouldn't get off the computer, Olivia decided the cat needed a shower and I had to rescue the poor thing, and Michael couldn't find his video game. We finally found it stuffed under a cushion on the couch." She plopped down on a chair. "Someone give me a cup of coffee before I totally wilt."

Molly jumped up and poured coffee into a mug. Handing it to Stephanie, she said, "I want to help with the investigation."

Stephanie pursed her lips. "You *are* helping. Taking care of the bookstore while we're gone is a tremendous help. It leaves us free to do what we have to do. "

"But I want to be *doing* something. I want to go with you."

Stephanie shook her head. "Not this time. We need you here."

Molly slumped down on the couch. "You guys have all the fun."

"It's not exactly fun," Clara said, getting up to put her mug down on the counter. "It could be dangerous."

Stephanie took another swallow of coffee and put down her mug. "Don't worry, Molly, we'll probably need you before this is over. We have to run now, so if you wouldn't mind washing the mugs for us, we'll take off so we can be back before the rush."

Molly sighed. "Okay . . . just be sure and tell me everything when you get back."

Stephanie answered her with a wave, and Clara followed her up the aisle to the front door. "Who shall we hit first, the motel manager or Buzz Lamont?" Stephanie asked as they stepped outside.

"The motel, I think." Clara started walking down the hill at a fast pace. "Let's hope the manager's not too busy to talk to us."

They reached the parking lot and decided to take Clara's car. Passing the harbor, she headed out along the coast road with the windows down to make the most of the clean, salty air. There were a lot of things she missed about New York, but the city smog wasn't one of them.

Stephanie chattered on about her kids and George, and Clara was content just to listen, until Stephanie said quietly, "You're worried about Rick, aren't you."

Clara sent her a startled look. "Of course I am. Aren't you?"

"Well, yes, but not in the way you are." She paused, then added, "Are you finally getting fond of him?"

Clara let out a short laugh. "Only as a friend, so you don't have to worry about that."

"I'm not worried. In fact, I'd worry less if you *were*

getting interested in Rick. You've seemed so . . . sad ever since you moved back from New York."

"Sad?" Clara shook her head. "I'm not sad. It's taken me a while to get used to living back here, that's all. I miss some of the things about my old life."

"Including the guy who dumped you?"

"Ouch." Clara took a deep breath. "No, he's one of the things I definitely don't miss." It was true, she realized. She still thought of him now and then. After all, she'd planned to spend the rest of her life with Matt. But she didn't miss him. Not anymore.

"Well, good. I thought maybe you were still hung up on the guy and that was stopping you from getting into a new relationship."

Clara shot her another glance. "Why the interest in my love life all of a sudden?"

Stephanie shrugged. "I don't know. You're not getting any younger, and you get all twittery whenever Rick is around. I guess I was hoping you two would get together. Of course, now that he's accused of murder, perhaps it's just as well you're not in love with him."

Clara gripped the steering wheel. "If I were in love with him, that wouldn't make the slightest bit of difference. I'd know he was innocent, just like I know now." With relief she glimpsed the sign for the Windrift Motel coming up on her left. "We're here. Let's hope the manager's ready to talk to us."

The young woman behind the reception desk in the motel's lobby seemed reluctant to call the manager. "Mr.

Tyler is in a meeting," she explained when Clara asked to speak to him. "He won't be out for another hour or so."

"Tell him this is an emergency," Clara said, grabbing Stephanie's arm when she started walking away. "It's very important that we speak to him."

The woman hesitated. "Sam doesn't like me disturbing him."

Clara leaned over the counter and said softly, "It's about the murder of one of his customers."

The receptionist threw a scared look over her shoulder. "Are you from the police? Sam has already talked to Dan and Tim Rossi."

Clara decided she needed to come on strong if she and Stephanie were going to get anywhere. "Just tell him we need to talk to him. *Now*."

The woman jumped up from her chair. "All right, but don't blame me if he's pissed." She disappeared through a door behind her.

Stephanie grabbed Clara's arm. "What if he gets mad and throws us out?"

Clara didn't want to admit her heart was thumping loud enough to be heard. Growing up had its disadvantages. When she and Stephanie were kids, they were both fearless, charging into adventures without a thought for the consequences. Now they were adults, with responsibilities, and dabbling with danger didn't seem nearly as much fun as it had all those years ago.

"Don't worry," she said, trying to sound more confident

than she felt, "We'll charm him into telling us what we want to know."

"What *do* we want to know?" Stephanie threw a fearful glance at the door behind the counter. "Have you thought about what to ask him?"

She hadn't. She'd figured it would come to her when she was actually talking to the man. If she were honest with herself, she'd admit she'd been hoping the Sense would chime in and let her know what she should say. She made herself smile. "I'll just ask him what he knows about Frank Tomeski."

The door opened suddenly, making them both jump. A skinny man with bowed shoulders and a scraggly beard peered at them through rimless glasses. "What do you want?" he barked, still holding on to the door handle.

It wasn't a very promising beginning, and Clara's smile was somewhat wobbly. "I'm so sorry to disturb you, Mr. Tyler. I promise we won't keep you long."

Tyler scowled at her. "Jenny says you're asking about the murder. You reporters or something? Because if so, I don't talk to no newspapers. Not without being paid, anyhow."

"We're not reporters." Clara looked over her shoulder as the main door to the lobby swung open. "Is there somewhere we can talk?"

The manager looked about to refuse, but just then Stephanie crept up to the counter and said in a voice reminiscent of Marilyn Monroe, "It's a personal matter, sir. We'd be *so* grateful if you could help us." She flashed him a smile and fluffed her hair with her fingers. "It would mean so very much to us."

Tyler looked a little less threatening. He walked to the end of the counter and lifted the flap. "You've got five minutes."

"Oh, thank you, sir," Stephanie murmured as she slipped past him.

Clara followed her, trying not to roll her eyes.

Sam Tyler led them into a small office and sat down at a cluttered desk, waving them to a couple of beat-up kitchen chairs. Swiping a pile of papers aside, he leaned back in his chair and stared at Clara. "So, what's this all about?"

Clara made herself meet his gaze. "It's about the murder of Frank Tomeski. A personal friend of ours is involved, and we're trying to find out what happened that night. We were hoping that you could help us."

There was a long silence while Tyler studied her, his eyebrows raised. Unnerved by the scrutiny, Clara cleared her throat. "Anything you can tell us about Mr. Tomeski might be helpful."

"You're a friend of Rick Sanders?" Tyler said at last.

Clara nodded. "I work in the bookstore opposite his hardware store. My cousin owns the bookstore."

"That's me!" Stephanie piped up, then huddled back on her chair as Tyler's sharp gaze sliced across her face.

"Anyway," Clara said, after sending a warning glance at her cousin, "we know that Rick didn't kill that man, and the police haven't had any luck finding who did do it, so we thought we'd give it a shot."

Tyler's eyes swiveled in her direction again. "Does Dan know about this?"

"Er . . . we haven't exactly discussed it with him." Clara gave him another wavering smile. "We just thought we'd ask some questions, that's all."

The manager seemed to be thinking it over, while Clara sat listening to her heartbeat thudding in her ears. She was hoping to hear voices telling her what to say next, but as had happened so often in the past, the Sense seemed to have deserted her.

Finally Tyler spoke, making her jump again. "Never did think Rick was a killer. I'll tell you what I told Dan. There was a young gal came looking for Tomeski while he was staying here. I sent her over to the Laurel Street Tavern. I'd seen Tomeski in there earlier and figured he'd still be there. She seemed real anxious to see him, and judging from the way she spoke, I'd say she wasn't planning on giving him a warm welcome when she saw him, if you know what I mean."

Clara leaned forward. "She was mad at him?"

"Mad as a hornet." Tyler sat up and reached for the phone on his desk. "Reckon she was ready to tell him a thing or two when she caught up with him. When I went in there the next night, I heard there'd been a big ruckus the night before, involving Tomeski and a bunch of other guys. I wouldn't be surprised if his girlfriend started it."

"Did she tell you her name?"

"Nope, and that's all I've got to say on the subject." He lifted the receiver. "Except this. Murder is a dangerous business. Especially for young women who don't know what they're doing. It's best left to the cops. That's their job, and I wouldn't want to see you two getting hurt or worse. Now get out of here. I've got a call to make."

Thanking him, Clara got to her feet and led Stephanie out to the foyer. The receptionist gave them a hard look as they walked briskly across the lobby to the main door.

Once outside, Clara let her shoulders relax. "Well, that was interesting," she said as she unlocked her car. "I'd say we have another suspect in the case."

Stephanie frowned. "She can't be much of a suspect. That manager had already told Dan what he told us, so Dan must know about her."

"He might know about her, but that doesn't mean he knows who she is." Clara slid into the car and waited for her cousin to get in.

Stephanie scrambled onto the seat and grabbed the seat belt. Clicking it into place, she said, "We don't know who that woman is, either."

"Not right now, we don't." Clara started the engine. "How would you like to spend an hour or so at the Laurel Street Tavern tonight?"

"Well, I guess a glass of beer on a hot night could be very refreshing."

Clara grinned at her. "My thoughts exactly."

"We could invite Molly along. You know what they say—there's safety in numbers."

Clara decided to ignore her doubts about including the young woman in their investigation. "All right. What about George? Will he mind if you go out again tonight?"

Stephanie made a face. "I'll tell him we're treating Molly to celebrate her birthday or something." She sighed. "I do hate lying to him. He'd go berserk if he knew the truth, though."

"Well, if we pay for Molly's beer, it will only be a half lie."

"I guess so." Stephanie peered gloomily ahead at the road. "I just hope we can find out enough to prove Rick is innocent. Then maybe all this will be worth it."

"Of course it will be worth it." Clara nodded at the road. "There's Belgrave Landscaping. Let's hope Buzz Lamont is there."

"Surrounded by a bunch of people."

Clara had to agree with her. She pulled off the road onto a gravel parking lot, the tires crunching on the small stones as she drove up to the main brick building. All along one side of the parking lot, rows of glasshouses glinted in the sun. In front of the building, stacks of bedding plants sheltered under a canopy, from which hung rows of hanging planters brimming with purple, pink and white fuchsias and red nasturtiums.

"Oh, they're so pretty!" Stephanie exclaimed, gazing at the planters as she climbed out of the car. "I have to take one home with me!"

"Good idea." Clara locked the car and took her cousin's arm as she headed for the door. "We can use it as an excuse to talk to someone."

The aroma in the cool interior of the building was a strange mix of sweet-smelling blooms and pungent fertilizer. Clara marched up to the long counter, where a couple of young men wearing brown coats were serving customers.

Stephanie darted over to a display of hanging planters and rushed back a moment later carrying a large container of blooms. "This will look lovely on my front porch," she said, dumping the planter on the counter.

One of the young men spotted her and came forward, smiling a welcome. "Can I help you?"

"I'll take this one." Stephanie fished in her fanny pack for her credit card and handed it over.

"Very nice," the assistant said, giving Stephanie an obvious look of admiration.

While he rang up the charge, Clara leaned on the counter. "I think a friend of ours works here," she said. "Buzz Lamont. Do you know him?"

The assistant barely looked at her, his gaze skimming past her to settle on Stephanie again. "Buzz? Sure I know him. He's a great guy."

"Is he here now? We'd love to say hello to him."

"He's out on a job." He handed Stephanie the slip to sign.

Clara waited until her cousin had handed back the pen before nudging her with her elbow. Stephanie shot her a puzzled glance, and Clara jerked her head at the assistant.

The young man handed Stephanie the receipt. "Hope you enjoy the flowers."

"Oh, I will." She buried her nose in the blooms, then smiled up at him. "I'd really like to see Buzz this morning. Would it be possible to stop by wherever he's working?"

The assistant leaned his elbows on the counter. "What is it worth to you if I tell you where he is?"

Clara saw her cousin's mouth tighten and quickly nudged her again.

Stephanie recovered her smile. "I could come see you again and buy some more flowers."

The young man's grin revealed a row of whitened teeth. "Deal. Hang on a minute." He disappeared down an aisle and after a tense wait, returned, waving a piece of paper.

"Here's where he's at," he said, handing it to Stephanie. "How about meeting me for a cup of coffee later to thank me?"

"I'll ask my husband. I'm sure he'd love to come along." Stephanie picked up the planter, turned her back on him and marched to the door.

Following her, Clara couldn't help grinning. "You made quite a conquest back there," she said, holding the car door open for her cousin.

"Idiot," Stephanie muttered, heaving the heavy basket onto the backseat. "He had to be half my age."

"Old enough to appreciate a gorgeous woman, obviously."

Stephanie straightened and climbed into the car. "Thanks a bunch, but right now I'm in no mood for flattery. I just hope that wherever Buzz Lamont is working, there are plenty of people around to keep him company."

"Well, I guess we'll find out." Clara started the engine again. "So what's the address?"

Stephanie read it out to her. "I think it's on the south side of town." She let out a shaky sigh. "I'm beginning to have second thoughts about this."

"Don't worry." Clara nosed the car across the gravel once more and onto the road. "If there's the slightest chance that he could hurt us, we'll find some other way to talk to him. Let's just take a look and see where he is, okay?"

"Okay." Stephanie settled down on her seat. "I should have brought the GPS with me. I don't know why you don't have one."

"I don't do that much driving."

"You drive all over town looking at apartments. Or at least, you used to look at them. You haven't done much of that lately."

"I guess I've given up trying to find something I like and can afford." Clara paused at a light. "Most of the rentals in town are vacation homes."

"Can't you use the Quinn Sense to find what you want?"

Clara sighed. "It doesn't work that way. Even if it did, I wouldn't use it."

Several minutes later she turned down a street and peered at the house numbers. "It should be down here somewhere. Ah, here it is. Look, there's one of Belgrave's trucks parked in the driveway."

Stephanie peered out the window as Clara parked the car. "It looks like a big house."

"Yeah, it does." Clara opened the door and climbed out. Two large wrought iron gates barred the entrance to the driveway, with tall shrubs on either side. A low brick wall ran across the front of the property and down each side, separating the yard from the houses on either side. The wide driveway curved up to an impressive front porch and verandah that circled the house. "Nice," Clara murmured, staring through the bars of the gate. "Very nice. We can't just walk in here. Not without a good excuse, anyway."

Stephanie stepped closer to look through the gate. "I can't see a gardener. Let's take a look farther down."

Clara followed close on her cousin's heels as she made her way along the wall. Stephanie stopped every yard or so and jumped up in an attempt to see over it. Clara didn't need to jump and for once was grateful for her height as she peered over the wall at an expanse of lawn with a water fountain in the middle of it. Shrubs lined the walls, but there was no sign of any gardeners.

"We have to get in the backyard," Stephanie declared

as they reached the end of the wall. "Buzz must be back there."

"How are we going to do that?" Clara gestured at the house. "We'd have to go up the driveway. Someone's bound to see us."

"We'll have to come up with an excuse to be here. Like we're Avon ladies or something."

"Wait!" Clara went back to her car and leaned in to reach the glove compartment. She found what she was looking for—a notebook and pen—and carried them back to her cousin. "I used this as an excuse to find out where Buzz worked," she said as Stephanie raised her eyebrows. "I told his wife I was conducting a survey."

"What kind of survey?"

"I don't know. Something about politics. I just told her it would be beneficial for him."

"Oh, great." Stephanie frowned. "He might think it odd that we tracked him down at work to ask him questions for a survey."

"Not him, silly. I mean if the owner or someone else sees us. We can tell them that's why we're here."

"Oh." Stephanie considered it. "Might work, but you have to know what it's about." She frowned some more, then her face cleared. "Let's say we're asking people's opinions about the economy. That always gets people talking."

Clara wasn't too sure about that but couldn't think of a better idea. Carefully, she opened the gate and stepped inside the yard. The muffled sound of deep barking made her pause. "There's a dog around somewhere."

Stephanie looked around. "I can't see one. Just keep going."

Clutching the pad to her chest, Clara walked up the driveway. The barking grew louder, though still muffled, and she thought it might be coming from inside the house. Quickening her step, she headed across the lawn to skirt the front windows.

She had just reached the far wall when a man in green coveralls stepped out in front of her. Startled, she dropped the pad and bent to retrieve it, while Stephanie came to a halt at her side. Straightening, Clara looked at the "Belgrave" badge sewn into the man's uniform. She gave him a smile. "Would you happen to be Buzz Lamont?"

The man's thin features stiffened with suspicion. "Who's asking?"

Stephanie eased back a step, unsettling Clara. Maybe they were taking too much of a chance confronting a possible killer. It was too late now, however. They were face-to-face with Buzz Lamont, and the chain saw in his hand was a formidable lethal weapon.

9

Clara pulled in a deep breath. "My name is Clara Quinn," she said quickly, "and I'm a friend of Rick Sanders."

The man's frown intensified. "Is that supposed to mean something to me?"

Clara felt Stephanie's fingers stabbing her in the back. Ignoring her she answered, "He's the man accused of killing Frank Tomeski."

The gardener's expression grew hostile. "What's that got to do with me?"

"I believe you were acquainted with Mr. Tomeski."

"Who told you that?"

Clara lifted her chin. "Never mind who told me. Is it true?"

"Are you a cop?"

Clara shook her head. "No, Mr. Lamont. I told you,

I'm just a friend of Rick Sanders. I'm trying to find out what I can about Frank Tomeski, because I don't believe Rick killed him. I'd be very grateful if you could tell me what, if anything, you know about him."

The gardener tilted his head to one side and studied her for a minute, then looked at Stephanie. "What about her?"

"She's my cousin. We work together in her bookstore. She's helping me find out what happened the night Frank Tomeski was killed."

Stephanie stepped forward, holding out a hand that wasn't quite steady. "I'm pleased to meet you."

Lamont stared at her as if she'd lost her mind. "What do you want to know?"

Clara moved closer to the wall to get out of the sun's searing glare. The barking had stopped. She hoped that meant the dog had settled down again and wasn't roaming around the yard looking for them. Stephanie scuttled over to join her, watched closely by the gardener.

"When did you last see Frank Tomeski?"

"About five years ago." Lamont shifted his position so he had his back to the sun. His skin had been burned to leather, and his light blue eyes seemed like twin laser beams as they raked Clara's face.

"Was he coming here to see you?" Clara watched him closely, hoping to read something in his face that would tell her if he was lying, since it seemed the Sense was absent as usual.

For a long moment she was afraid he wasn't going

to answer, then he seemed to make up his mind about something and shook his head. "I didn't even know Frank was in town until I saw his face on TV. I'd been at the shooting range for a couple of hours, and I went over to the bowling alley for a beer or two. That's when Frank turned up on the news. Believe me, that was some kind of shock."

"It must have been a bigger shock to realize you were in the bowling alley the night he was killed."

Buzz narrowed his eyes. "You been talking to Jason? He needs his mouth sewn up with catgut."

Clara hurried on. "Do you remember anything about that night that might have seemed unusual? Like someone acting weird?"

"The only thing I remember about that night is nearly being run over by a black SUV. If I hadn't stepped out the way pretty quick, I would have ended up next to Frank in the morgue."

"How well did you know Frank?"

Buzz shrugged. "Not that well. We used to do business together when I lived in Portland."

"What kind of business?"

The gardener pursed his lips. "Personal business."

Clara let that go. "Did you keep in touch with him after you left Portland?"

"Now and then. Not a lot. We'd exchange e-mails once in a while. Frank didn't have many friends."

"So you have no idea who he might have been meeting when he came here."

Buzz uttered a short laugh. "I can guess. I reckon he was here meeting some bimbo he picked up online. He was always chatting with women on the Internet. Sent me a pic now and then. I always figured he'd get into trouble one day over some woman. If you ask me, I'd say a jealous boyfriend or husband whacked him."

Clara let out her breath. "Why didn't you tell all this to the police? You must have seen their announcements on TV asking if anyone knew the victim."

Buzz stuck his hands in his pockets. "Not that it's any of your business, but I didn't call the cops because I've got a record. The cops are quick to jump on ex-cons. I've been straight for six years now. I've got a good job, and a wife and family. If news got out about my past, I could kiss all that good-bye." He took a step toward Clara, making Stephanie scrunch up closer to the wall. "If you so much as breathe one word of this to anyone else, I'll make you sorry you ever set eyes on me."

Clara held up her hands. "I'm not going to tell anyone anything. I just want to find out what happened that night and clear Rick's name."

Seemingly satisfied, Buzz drew back. "You might want to look at Frank's girlfriend, Stella Wilkins. He's been dating her on and off for ten years. I can understand why he never married her. She's a bad-tempered witch. Thinks she owns him. I can just imagine what she'd do if she found out Frank was down here banging some dame. Probably kill them both."

Clara was about to answer when a low growl made her

freeze. Glancing at the corner of the house, she saw a fierce-looking German shepherd, legs braced apart, head lowered, teeth bared and growling.

"Oh crap," Stephanie said, sounding as if she were about to cry.

"Lay down, King," Buzz Lamont said sharply.

The dog stopped growling and raised his head, though he still stared at the Clara with a warning in his eyes.

Clara held out her hand and started toward the dog.

"I wouldn't do that if I were you," Buzz said, sounding worried. "That dog's got a mean streak."

Clara kept moving slowly toward the dog. "It's all right, boy," she said softly. "We're leaving."

The dog pushed his nose forward and sniffed her hand, then sat, his gaze still watchful on her face.

"Let's go, Stephanie." Clara gently laid a hand on the dog's head. "Thank you, Mr. Lamont, for all your help. I promise you, no one will know you spoke to us. Good luck with everything."

Stephanie hurried past her and headed down the driveway without looking back.

Clara gave the dog a final pat on the head, then walked after her cousin.

She had gone just a few steps when Buzz called out, "Good luck to you, too. Sanders is a lucky guy."

She waved in answer, smiling to herself as she followed Stephanie out of the gate.

"So, do you think he did it?" Stephanie asked as they drove back down the lane.

Clara frowned. "I don't know. He seemed to be telling the truth, but it was hard to tell."

"So what happened to the Quinn Sense?"

"The same thing that happens most of the time. I told you it was unpredictable."

Stephanie slumped back in her seat. "We're no closer to finding out who killed Frank Tomeski. No wonder Dan is having so much trouble solving this murder."

Clara pulled onto the highway and sped up. "We have Frank's girlfriend's name. That might help."

"How? She lives in Portland. Are you planning on going there to find her?"

Clara shrugged. "Not yet. I think we should go down to the tavern tonight and talk to the bartender. I'd like to know what happened when Stella Wilkins caught up with Frank in there."

"Do you think we should tell Dan who she is?"

Clara thought about it. "If we do that," she said at last, "we'd have to tell him about Buzz Lamont. If Buzz was telling the truth, and he's really worried about losing his wife or his job, or both, I really don't want to be the one who causes all that."

"What if he's not telling the truth? What if he killed Frank Tomeski and told you a bunch of lies to throw suspicion on someone else?"

Clara shrugged. "I guess we'll find out eventually. In the meantime, I'd really like to talk to someone at the tavern about that fight."

"Okay." Stephanie glanced at the clock. "Oh crap, look

at the time. The Reading Nook will be packed by now. Molly must have her hands full."

"We'll be there in five minutes." Clara put some pressure on the accelerator. Her mind was already forging ahead to that evening, rehearsing the questions she would ask. One thing she'd learned from her sparse investigative experience: people were inclined to tell her things they wouldn't tell the police. Between that and the elusive Quinn Sense, she was hopeful they would uncover enough solid evidence to set Dan on the track of the real killer.

When they arrived at the Raven's Nest a few minutes later, it was to find Molly dashing out of the Nook, her red hair flying around her flushed face. Clara muttered a quick apology and got to work serving the two customers waiting at the counter.

The next hour or so went by quickly as they all washed mugs, refilled the coffeepot and served up donuts and Danish. When the last customer walked out the door, Molly leaned on the counter with a sigh. "That was crazy. We haven't been that busy since we opened the Reading Nook."

Stephanie grinned. "Isn't that great? I just love the summer and all the tourists. We did really well in sales so far today."

Clara patted her on the back. "You'd better get going. Your kids are probably wondering where you are."

Stephanie made a face. "They're probably making the most of the extra time with Grandma. You're right, I'd better get over there before things get out of hand." She darted over to the door, calling out over her shoulder, "Tell Molly about tonight, okay? I haven't had a chance to talk to her." With that, she was gone.

Molly raised her eyebrows at Clara. "Tonight?"

Clara sighed. "Stephanie and I are going to the tavern on Laurel Street this evening. We thought you might like to come along."

Molly's eyes lit up. "Are we investigating?"

"Sort of." Clara filled her in on the events of the morning, while Molly's eyes grew wider as the story progressed.

"Wow," she muttered, when Clara was finished. "You two sound just like those detectives on TV."

Clara laughed. "Which ones?"

Molly waved a hand in the air. "All of them! Weren't you scared when you saw Buzz Lamont holding a chain saw?"

"A little, I guess." Clara walked over to the table where an untidy stack of cookbooks lay and started straightening them. "We were taking a chance, but this is about a murder, and we're not going to solve it without taking a few chances."

"I guess not." Molly sounded subdued. "Do you think it will be dangerous tonight?"

"Not really. We'll be in a crowded place, and there will be three of us. As long as we stick together and don't get separated, we should be just fine."

Molly hugged her arms. "This is exciting. I've got goose bumps!"

Clara walked over to her. "Let's not forget why we're doing this. Rick's whole future could be on the line. It's important we get as much information as we can, without upsetting anyone. Okay?"

Molly nodded. "Okay! What time are we going?"

"You and Stephanie can go when you like. I have to close up here, so it'll be around eight fifteen by the time I get there."

"I'll call Stephanie later and find out what time she wants to go. I can't wait!"

"Whatever you do," Clara warned, "don't start asking questions without me."

Molly grinned. "Don't worry, we'll wait for you."

Clara left her and walked down to the Nook to clean up after the coffee crowd. She still wasn't too comfortable about Molly coming with them to the tavern, though she wasn't sure why. Maybe it was because Molly was a few years younger than the cousins, and a little more impulsive, though what harm that could do, Clara wasn't sure.

Deciding that she was being way too negative about the whole thing, she put the thought out of her mind and concentrated instead on cleaning up the Nook.

Halfway through the afternoon, just as Clara was about to take a ten-minute break, her cell phone rang and her mother's voice screeched in her ear. "Did you not take this dog out for a walk before you left for work this morning?"

Tatters! Clara slapped a hand over her mouth. She'd

completely forgotten about the dog. "Oh, poor thing! Is he all right?"

"He's perfectly fine. I, on the other hand, am definitely not all right. If you'd seen the mess I had to pick up just now, neither would you be."

Clara rolled her eyes at the ceiling. "I'm so sorry. I had errands to run this morning and didn't have time to get back to the house before I had to start work."

"Well, I refuse to come home to this disgusting mess again. The next time I walk in here and find it like this, I will simply turn around and walk right out again and leave it for you to clean up. If this is the best you can do in taking care of this animal, I suggest you find him a home with someone else."

Clara gripped the phone. Until then she hadn't realized how very much she would hate having to find another home for Tatters. "I'm sorry, Mother. I'll make sure it doesn't happen again, and if it does, I'll take care of it."

"You can be quite sure of that." Her mother paused, then added, "He needs a walk. You can take him when you get home."

Clara almost groaned out loud. "Er . . . I'm sorry, but I have to go out tonight. I should be home around ten or so. I don't suppose you could take him?"

"Are you out of your mind?" Jessie's voice had risen to a squeak. "If you think I'm going to let that huge beast drag me around the block, you had better think again. He can go when you get home tonight. Where are you going, anyway?"

Clara hesitated a bit too long. Her mother's angry voice rang in her ear. "All right, don't tell me. I don't know why you have to be so secretive about your life. I am your mother, you know."

"Stephanie and I are taking Molly out for a drink," Clara said, wondering why everything had to be so complicated. "I won't be late."

"Well, why didn't you say that in the first place?"

"I was going to, but you didn't give me a chance."

Jessie answered more quietly, "All right. I'll take the dog for a walk. Though heaven knows where he'll drag me."

Clara had to smile. "You know very well you can control that dog better than I can."

"If you say so." Jessie paused again. "Have fun."

Clara's smile turned rueful as she closed her cell phone and slipped it in her pocket.

She had to admit to feeling a little unnerved at the prospect of the trip to the tavern. Laurel Street was on the edge of town, and the tavern was notorious for drunken brawls and the occasional arrest. Not the kind of place she'd choose for an evening out. Definitely not the kind of place she should be taking a vulnerable young woman like Molly.

It was too late now, however. The plans had been set, and she could hardly back out now. Putting her doubts aside, she joined Molly at the counter. "You might as well take off," she said, glancing at the clock. "Your shift is almost over, and there's not much going on here."

Molly wasted no time in grabbing her purse and

heading for the door. "See you around eight!" she called out and disappeared into the street.

Left alone, Clara wandered down the aisles, checking the shelves for books that were out of order or otherwise misplaced. She was at the far end of the store when she heard the front doorbell ring. Welcoming the distraction, she hurried to the front of the shop to greet the customer.

Her pulse jumped a little when she saw Rick standing by the cookbook table, his gaze concentrated on the heavy volume in his hands. Immediately reminded of her cousin accusing her of being twittery around him, she made an effort to sound indifferent. "See anything you like?"

He looked up at her, his gray eyes brimming with laughter. "Definitely. This cookbook looks interesting, too."

Much to her annoyance, she felt her cheeks warm, and she rushed over to the counter, hoping he wouldn't notice. "It just came in a few days ago. Knowing how much you like to cook, I knew you'd appreciate that book."

"I see it has a number of recipes from northern Italy." He turned a couple of pages. "My favorite kind of Italian cooking."

"There's a difference?"

He closed the book and walked over to the counter. "A big difference. Northern Italian cuisine doesn't rely on tomato sauce like the cooking in central and southern Italy does. The northern Italians use chopped herbs in wine or broth for their sauces."

"Mmm. I think I like it."

He grinned. "I'll have to cook a northern Italian meal for you sometime. I still owe you for taking Tatters off my hands. How are things going, by the way? No major catastrophes, I hope?"

Clara closed her mind against the picture of her mother cleaning up after the dog. "Tatters is a sweetheart and he's behaving like a gentleman."

Rick frowned. "We are talking about the same dog, aren't we?"

Clara laughed. "You wouldn't know him. He's settled down just fine."

"Amazing. Someday you'll have to tell me how you managed that."

She wondered what he'd say if she told him about her unusual abilities "I told you, he just needed attention, that's all." Before he could answer, she changed the subject. "How are things going with you?"

His expression changed at once, worrying her. His shrug didn't quite hide the tension in his face as he said, "Okay, I guess. If you don't mind being treated like you have some terrible contagious disease."

"Oh, Rick, I'm so sorry."

His smile returned, though his eyes reflected his misery. "I keep hoping to hear Dan say he's caught the murderer and locked him up in jail. I just want to get my life back the way it was, before all this happened."

She felt angry at all those stupid, ignorant people who were so quick to judge. "Don't let some people get you down," she said, knowing that her words couldn't possibly take away the pain. "They'll be the ones feeling bad when they learn the truth."

"If they ever learn the truth." He put the book down on the counter and reached in his back pocket for his wallet. "I'm beginning to think I'm doomed to be treated like an outcast for the rest of my life, always under suspicion and never trusted again." He pulled a credit card from his wallet and handed it to her. "I may have to sell up and move out."

"No!" She'd sounded more devastated than she'd intended and quickly turned away from him to ring up the charge. "I'd hate to see you do that," she added more calmly. "Don't let a few blockheads drive you out of your home and business. Dan will find the killer, I know it."

"Well, until he does, I'm not allowed to leave town anyway, so it looks like I'm stuck."

She handed him back his card and the receipt. "Just hang in there. Not everyone thinks you're a murderer."

"Thanks." He took the card from her and tucked it in his pocket, while she bagged the book. "I guess it's at times like this you find out who your friends are."

"Absolutely." She held out the book. "And I know you have a lot of them."

"None quite as loyal as you." He headed for the door, saying over his shoulder, "Let's get together soon for a home-cooked Italian dinner."

"Just name the day." She watched him leave, feeling so sorry for him she could cry.

Ten minutes before she was ready to close up shop the

doorbell rang again. This time John Halloran stood leering at her as she approached the counter.

"I just stopped in to see if you've got anything new in the *Devil's World* series," he said, starting down one of the aisles. "I finished the last one I bought. Excellent book."

Clara decided to let him browse the shelves on his own. She was in no mood for his snide remarks. With one eye on the clock, she waited for him to return to the counter.

It was a minute or two past eight when he finally wandered out of the aisle, carrying a couple of books. "Sorry," he said with his sleazy smile. "It took me a while to make up my mind."

"It's okay." She took the books from him and rang up the charge.

"I saw Rick in here earlier." John hunched his shoulders. "He's having a hard time of it."

"Yes, he is," Clara said as she handed him his receipt.

"Did he say anything to you, about the investigation, I mean?" John's eyes gleamed at her from behind his glasses. "He doesn't say much to me."

"That's probably because there's not a lot to say." Clara bagged the books and handed them over. "He's waiting, like everyone else is, for the police to find the real murderer."

"So you don't think he did it."

Clara glared at him. "Of course he didn't do it. How can anyone believe that Rick Sanders is capable of murder?"

John nodded. "Of course, I heartily agree. But that means the killer is still on the loose around here. Unless he's left town. Maybe the police will never find out who did it." He headed for the door, pausing to look back at her as he reached it. "That would be a shame," he murmured. "That would be a great shame." Shaking his head, he went out the door and let it close behind him.

Clara frowned at the door, trying to figure out what the heck John meant by all that. He was an odd man, always talking in riddles, and there were times when she wondered if he was merely rambling or if he was deliberately trying to confuse everyone.

Glancing at the clock again, she walked quickly over to the door and turned the "Open" sign around to "Closed." She didn't have time to worry about John Halloran right now. It was well past eight and she had to get to Laurel Street. All she hoped was that they'd learn something—anything—that would help track down whoever had killed Frank Tomeski, and put an end to all the speculation. Maybe then she could look forward to an evening of home-cooked Italian food and good wine.

10

It took Clara several minutes longer than she'd expected to find the tavern on Laurel Street. She parked on the street, leery of leaving the car in the shadowed parking lot behind the building.

The tavern looked like an old shack, with tiny windows and a door that badly needed paint. Judging from the sound of raised voices and the heavy thumping of a bass guitar, there was no shortage of customers inside. The noise blasted her ears when she pushed the door open and walked in. The smell of beer and sweaty bodies almost made her turn around and walk out again, but she caught sight of Stephanie and Molly at a table by the window and headed in their direction.

Molly's cheeks were flushed, and she was clutching a

glass of beer in her hands as if afraid someone would snatch it away from her.

"How many has she had?" Clara demanded as she sat down at the table.

Stephanie rolled her eyes. "She's halfway through her first glass. We only just got here half an hour ago."

"I'm over twenty-one, anyway," Molly said, lifting the glass. "I'm allowed to drink as much as I want."

"Not as long as I'm sitting here." Clara caught her cousin's raised eyebrows. "I'm responsible for her being here. I'm not going to be responsible for her getting drunk. Unless you want to leave her car here and take her home yourself."

Molly put down the glass. "Take it easy, Clara. I'm not that crazy about beer, anyway. I'm just drinking it to be sociable."

Stephanie leaned forward. "Are you okay? You sound frazzled."

Clara sighed and leaned back on her chair. "Sorry. Between my mother and Tatters, and now this place, I'm beginning to feel a little fragile."

Stephanie burst out laughing. "Fragile? You? Never. Order a drink and you'll feel better."

Clara caught the eye of a buxom middle-aged blonde wearing a red T-shirt three sizes too small for her and jeans that strained at the seams. Her jaw worked at a piece of chewing gum as she took Clara's order. "We don't have no chardonnay," she said, scribbling down something on her pad. "We've just got white wine or red."

"That's why I'm drinking beer," Stephanie muttered.

Giving in to the inevitable, Clara ordered a beer. "I guess we should start asking questions."

"Are you going to question Miss America over there?" Stephanie nodded at their server, who was now leaning over the counter giving her order to the bartender.

Molly giggled, then straightened her face when Clara looked at her.

"We'll talk to the manager." Clara glanced around the crowded bar. "That's if this place has a manager."

"Here comes Blondie again," Stephanie said, nodding at the server crossing the room toward them. "We can ask her."

Clara waited while the woman took a beer off her loaded tray and dumped the glass down on the table. "You wanna tab?" The server nodded at Stephanie. "She's got one."

"Add it to hers, then." Clara smiled. "She's good for it."

The server looked at Stephanie, who nodded. About to turn away, the woman paused when Clara asked, "I'd like to speak to the manager. Is he here?"

The server spun around so fast beer slopped over the sides of the glasses on her tray. "Whatcha want to see the manager for? What did I do wrong?"

She looked so fierce Clara eased back on her chair. "You haven't done anything. I just want to talk to him about something else, that's all."

"Well, if you're looking for a job, I can tell you, we ain't hiring right now."

"I'm not looking for a job." Clara tried another smile. "I just want to ask the manager about something. Can you tell me where I can find him?"

"It ain't a *he*, it's a *her*." The blonde jerked her finger at the counter. "She's the redhead behind the bar."

"Figures," Stephanie muttered.

Clara nodded. "Thank you."

The server stood there for a moment longer, her face tight with suspicion, then she marched off to serve the rest of her customers.

"Wow," Molly said, watching her leave, "she's one tough cookie."

"Take a look at the manager," Stephanie said, nodding at the bar. "She makes Miss America look like a librarian."

Clara followed her cousin's gaze and finally focused on the redhead. The manager's bright red hair was cropped close to her head, and her eyes were ringed with black, giving her the look of a belligerent raccoon. Her arms bulged beneath the short sleeves of her black T-shirt, and she wore what looked like a studded dog collar around her throat.

"Holy crap," Stephanie said as she watched the woman playfully cuff one of her customers behind the ear. "I wouldn't want to get her mad at me."

Clara swallowed. The longer she stayed in that noisy, smelly place, the less enthusiastic she got about asking questions. She would give anything to be outside, breathing in fresh sea air. The memory of Rick's unhappy face, however, revived her. Someone had to help him, and it didn't look as if anyone else was rushing to his aid.

She swallowed a couple of mouthfuls of beer and put the glass down. "Wish me luck."

Stephanie looked startled. "You want us to come with you?"

"No. She might be more willing to talk if she's not facing three of us."

"Okay, but we'll be watching, just in case."

"In case of what?" Molly asked, sounding worried.

"In case she needs help." Stephanie smiled at her. "It's okay. I'm sure she'll be just fine."

Wishing she could feel as confident, Clara walked over to the bar. The redhead was deep in conversation with a burly guy whose nose looked as if it had been broken more than once. Clara leaned one elbow on the counter and tried to look as if this were her usual choice of evening entertainment.

She'd have felt better if she'd been wearing a T-shirt and jeans—apparently the uniform for patrons of the Laurel Street Tavern—instead of the ruffled top and slacks she'd worn to work.

A male voice jerked her out of her thoughts, and she looked up to see a young bartender with greasy hair and an even greasier smile gazing at her as if she were about to offer him a thousand-dollar bonus. She glanced down to where the manager was still chatting to Broken Nose.

Deciding she might as well take advantage of the opportunity, she smiled back. "Hi, I'd like a white wine, please."

"Coming right up!" The bartender picked up a wineglass and twirled it in his fingers before setting it down on the counter. Clara watched with interest as he swung a bottle of wine up in the air. The devilish part of her was hoping he'd drop it, but he caught it deftly by the neck and set it down next to the glass.

His next trick was to throw a corkscrew over his head and catch it behind his back. When it landed in his fingers, he got a burst of applause from the several men seated at the bar. Clara resisted the urge to join in the clapping. The bartender looked disappointed. Apparently his performance had been solely for her benefit.

"Haven't seen you in here before," he said as he poured her a generous glass of wine.

"That's because I haven't been in here before." Clara sipped from the glass, doing her best not to make a face.

"You must be a tourist, then." The bartender wiped down the counter with a grubby-looking cloth.

"Nope." Clara put down the glass. "I live here."

The bartender's smile widened. "So, what's a nice girl like you doing in a place like this?"

Clara laughed. "Maybe I'm looking for some excitement. Someone told me you have plenty of action in here."

"Action?" The bartender raised his eyebrows. "What kind of action?"

"I can give you all the action you want," a voice said at her elbow.

Clara looked at the bald-headed man grinning at her. "I didn't mean that kind of action." She turned back to the bartender. "I heard you had a big fight in here last week."

The bartender's expression changed. "I don't know nothing about that." He gave her a hard look and walked away from her down the bar.

"I do," the bald-headed man said, sidling closer to her.

Clara edged away from him. "Were you here that night?"

The man nodded. "Jim's the name. Jim Hardy."

He held out his hand and Clara brushed it with her fingers. "Nice to meet you. So tell me about the fight."

It seemed Jim Hardy was eager to tell her what happened. He settled himself on the stool by her side and leaned forward, eyes gleaming. "I was right here at the counter when it started. This guy comes in, and you could tell right away he was looking for trouble. He was all tense and nervous, if you know what I mean. He ordered a double shot of Jim Beam and chucked it down his throat as if he hadn't had a drink in months. Then he orders another one and downs that, too." Jim shook his head. "I never saw anyone drink good bourbon that fast."

Clara shook her head. "That must have gone to his head in a hurry."

"I dunno. Some guys can drink a whole bottle before they get a buzz, if you know what I mean." Jim picked up his beer glass and guzzled some down. "Personally I can't touch the stuff. Kills my stomach."

Clara nodded in sympathy. "So what about the fight? "

"Yeah, well, this guy was on his fourth double when Jake Pritchard comes in with Vera, his girlfriend." He nodded at a group of men sitting near the door. "That's Jake over there. The big guy with the beard and shaggy eyebrows. That's Vera next to him. Those two have been going out together for years. I don't know why they don't up and get married."

"I'm sure they have their reasons," Clara said, thinking about what Buzz had said about Frank Tomeski's girlfriend. "So did the man at the bar start a fight with Jake?"

Jim nodded. "Went after his girlfriend. Vera came up to the bar to give their order. Jake always sends her up here when it's busy. He don't like to be kept waiting, that Jake. Tough bastard, he is."

Looking across the room at Jake, Clara was inclined to agree. "So what happened then?"

"Well, this guy goes up to Vera at the bar and tries to hit on her. Vera doesn't want none of it." He glanced across the room. "If you ask me, she's afraid of Jake. Can't say I blame her."

Out of the corner of her eye, Clara saw the bartender whispering something to the manager and nodding in her direction. It made her uneasy, and she tried to hurry up Jim's saga of the fight. "So Jake got jealous?" she prompted.

Jim grinned. "Not at first. He didn't see what was going on. It was this other gal who started everything. Must have been the guy's girlfriend. She came screaming in the door and rushed right over to the counter and grabbed

Vera's hair. She was yelling and cursing at the guy, while Vera was trying to get free from her. That's when Jake sees what's going on and comes rushing over. He threw a punch at the guy, and that's when I got out of here. I could tell what was going down, and I didn't want to be no part of it."

Clara glanced down the bar and saw the manager heading her way. "Well, thank you," she said, backing away from the counter. "It was nice talking to you."

Jim looked upset. "Hey, where are you going? I haven't told you the best part yet. The guy ended up dead in the back of someone's truck the next day. Talk about bad luck! I reckon—"

"Jim!"

The harsh voice cut off Jim's words. He spun around to face the redhead, who stood with arms folded, glaring at him. "That's enough talk, Jim," she said, throwing a lethal look at Clara. "You know I don't like gossip around here."

"I was just being friendly, Rosie," Jim said, his voice rising to a whine. "You know I don't mean any harm."

Clara didn't wait to hear the manager's response. She headed back to the table and sat down with her back to the counter.

"Who was that you were talking to?" Stephanie's face was creased with worry.

"Just some guy." Clara grabbed her beer and swallowed a couple of mouthfuls. "He was telling me all about the fight."

"Well, the manager doesn't look too happy. I think she's telling him off."

Clara resisted the impulse to turn around to look. "I don't think she liked him telling me about what happened."

"She's looking over here," Molly said. "I hope she's not going to throw us out."

Stephanie frowned at Molly, then turned back to her cousin. "What did the guy tell you, anyway?"

Clara repeated the whole conversation as best she could remember. "I'd really like to talk to Jake. I wonder how much they've told Dan about the fight. The bartender didn't want to talk about it, and it's obvious Rosie didn't want anyone saying anything about it."

Stephanie looked puzzled. "Rosie?"

"The manager." Clara picked up her glass again. "Is she still looking over here?"

"No, but I wouldn't go asking any more questions around here if I were you."

"I can!" Molly looked excited. "Let me ask Jake about the fight. Rosie won't notice me. She's not looking over here anymore. She's busy talking to those guys at the bar."

Clara glanced over to the table by the door. Jake was still there, talking to the other couple seated with him. His girlfriend, it seemed, had left the table. "I guess Vera's in the bathroom."

Stephanie frowned. "Who's Vera?"

"Jake's girlfriend." Clara nodded at the table.

"Well, now, here's your chance!" Stephanie jabbed her

with her elbow. "Go talk to the girlfriend in the bathroom. She'll probably tell you more than that brute over there, and Rosie won't see you asking questions."

Clara looked at her. "Why don't *you* go?"

"Because you're better at this than me. I'm the ideas person, remember?"

Clara pushed her chair back and got up. "I don't know why I listen to you."

"Because you know I'm right."

"Then why are we always getting into trouble?"

Stephanie grinned. "Because we like a little excitement in our life."

Shaking her head, Clara headed for the ladies' room. She found a "Women" sign on a door at the end of a long hallway and pushed it open.

Vera stood at the sink, peering into the mirror as she tweaked her spiky blonde hair. Her bare arms looked like sticks, and her orange tank top hung on her skinny frame. With the dark circles under her eyes and sunken cheeks, she looked like a refugee from a prison camp.

When Clara walked over to the sink next to her, she could smell nicotine on the woman's clothes. Turning on the faucet, she began washing her hands. She saw Vera's puzzled glance in the mirror and smiled at her. "Can't be too careful," she said cheerfully, lathering the liquid soap until it formed bubbles.

Vera's mouth twitched in a resemblance of a smile, and she turned to leave.

Clara stepped back at the same time and bumped into

her. "Oh, excuse me!" She peered into Vera's face. "Didn't I see you in here the other night? The night of the big fight?"

Vera's face turned white under her makeup, and her eyes grew wide. "I don't know what you're talking about."

"Yes, you do." Clara moved closer. She was several inches taller than the other woman and once again blessed her height. It helped to give her some authority. "I'm talking about the fight between your boyfriend Jake and Frank Tomeski."

Vera backed up against the wall. There was genuine fear on her face, and Clara felt terrible about intimidating the poor woman. She was about to apologize when Vera blurted out, "If you think my Jake killed that man you're dead wrong. The cops already talked to him, and I told them Jake was with me the night that guy got killed—*all* that night. We went straight home from here, and we never went out again until the next morning."

Clara puffed out her breath. "Okay, I'm sorry I—"

"If you wanna know, ask the dead guy's girlfriend. She's a real mean bitch, and with a temper like hers it wouldn't surprise me if she'd clobbered him." With that, Vera pushed past her and rushed out the door.

Clara's hands shook as she dried them on a paper towel. She'd never been very good at asserting herself, and bullying definitely wasn't her style. Vera had seemed scared to death, though maybe part of her fear stemmed from her relationship with her boyfriend. Even so, Clara felt guilty. This investigative work was a lot harder than it seemed.

She left the bathroom and headed back to her table. On the way she saw Vera talking earnestly to Jake and nodding in her direction. Sensing trouble, Clara hurried over to her table and grasped Stephanie's arm. "Come on," she said, jerking her head at Molly. "We're leaving."

"I haven't finished my beer," Molly complained.

Out of the corner of her eye, Clara saw Jake standing up. "Let's get out of here. *Now!*" She tugged so hard Stephanie let out a yelp of pain.

Both women stood, but by then, Jake was heading in their direction.

"Now what?" Clara muttered.

Stephanie uttered a soft, "Oh crap," while Molly simply looked scared.

Clara squared her shoulders. "I'll handle this. Just let me do the talking."

She sat down again and signaled the others to do the same. It seemed less provoking somehow.

Jake looked even bigger as he loomed over her. His face was set in stone, and the look in his eyes sent a shiver of fear down her spine. "My girlfriend said you were asking her questions about the fight the other night."

She tried to smile, but her mouth seemed to be frozen. "I . . . was just making conversation."

He leaned in closer until she could smell the beer on his breath. "That's not the way I heard it."

Before she could answer him, Molly jumped up and rushed around the table. "I know you," she said, her voice rising in excitement. "You're that new rapper I saw on that TV talent show!"

Jake straightened, confusion all over his face. "What? Lady, I think you've got me—"

Molly didn't let him finish. "You were so *good*! I just *knew* you were going to win. Can I please have your autograph?"

Jake shook his head. "Listen, I'm not—"

She tugged at his sleeve. "Oh, *please*? I'd just die if you don't give it to me!" She snatched up the menu off the table. "Here, you can sign this." She turned to Clara, who was still trying to figure out what was going on. "He's an awesome rapper. You've just got to hear him."

Jake took a step backward. "I'm trying to tell you, lady, I'm not—"

Molly leapt toward him. "Oh, please, do one for us now! The one you did on stage. We'd just love to hear it again, wouldn't we, girls?"

Stephanie nodded.

"Love to," Clara managed weakly.

Molly turned to the next table, where a group of young women were all watching Jake with great interest. "You should hear this guy. He's *phenomenal*!" She spun around to face Jake again. "Come on, mister! We're all waiting, aren't we?"

The women nodded and one of them started clapping.

Molly joined in and several other people started applauding.

Clara felt an urge to laugh as Jake's face turned red. He muttered something under his breath and glared at Molly. "Get out of my way, you crazy nutcase."

Molly quickly shifted to one side, and Jake took off, head bowed as the applause followed him all the way to his table.

"Let's go," Clara said, snatching a couple of bills from her purse. She dropped them on the table and headed for the door, followed closely by Stephanie and Molly.

Once outside, she leaned against the door of her car and let out her breath. "That was a close one."

Stephanie tucked her arm in Molly's. "That was fantastic. Whatever made you think of that?"

Molly shrugged. "I saw someone do it in a TV movie. I thought it was worth a shot."

"Well, it worked, thank goodness." Stephanie looked at her cousin. "Whatever did you say to that woman in the bathroom?"

Clara shook her head. "Nothing much. Actually she did all the talking. She said that Jake was with her the night Frank Tomeski was killed."

"And you believe her?"

Clara pursed her lips. "I don't know. I don't know who to believe anymore. Everyone we talk to seems to have a reason to be mad at Frank Tomeski, but I don't know if any of it was enough to kill him."

"Maybe whoever attacked him didn't mean to kill him," Molly said, sounding subdued. "Maybe he or she just wanted to teach him a lesson and it got out of hand."

"That could be," Stephanie agreed. "The killer probably panicked and threw the body in the closest hiding place—Rick's truck."

"Well, whoever it was, it doesn't look as if we're going to find him. Or her." Clara looked gloomily down the street. "We suck at this."

Stephanie patted her arm. "No we don't. If Dan can't find out who the killer is, what chance do we have? You've done your best, Clara. I guess we just have to leave it up to the police to solve the case."

"Meanwhile, Rick is under suspicion everywhere he goes." Clara shook her head. "I can't leave it like this. I just can't. I have to keep trying."

"We've run out of people to ask," Stephanie said, her face serious under the streetlamp. "If one of the people we've already questioned did it, I don't see how we can prove anything."

"We haven't talked to Stella Wilkins yet." Clara saw Stephanie's frown and added, "Frank Tomeski's girl-friend."

"Oh, right." Stephanie laid a hand on her arm. "You're not going to Portland to find her, are you? Why don't you just tell Dan her name and let him question her?"

"I don't know if Dan *can* question her if she's out of his jurisdiction."

"Then let Dan worry about that. There must be some way he can get to her."

Clara rubbed her eyes. "I have to get home. Tatters is probably locked up in the utility room by now and making all kinds of noise. I'll worry about all this in the morning."

Stephanie still looked concerned. "Promise you won't do anything rash without talking to me first?"

Clara smiled. "I'm not exactly a rash person, remember?"

"Oh, I don't know. You've had your moments." She turned to Molly. "Did I ever tell you about the time—"

"I'm going home," Clara said firmly and opened the car door. "And if you don't want Jake to come storming out here after you, I suggest you both do the same."

Molly sent a fearful glance at the tavern door. "You're right. See you in the morning!"

She started toward the edge of the building, and Stephanie called out after her. "Wait for me! We parked in the back," she added as Clara climbed into her car.

"Then be careful." Clara fastened her seat belt. "Don't hang around back there."

Stephanie nodded and took off after Molly. Puffing out her breath, Clara turned the key and started the engine. They had spent the entire day and evening asking questions, and in spite of what they'd learned, they were no closer to figuring out who had killed Frank Tomeski. It was frustrating, to say the least.

Driving down the highway, she went over in her mind

everything she'd heard that day. There had to be a clue somewhere in all that, but for the life of her she couldn't think what it might be. Maybe tomorrow, after a good night's sleep, she'd be able to see things more clearly.

What bothered her the most was knowing she was letting Rick down. If she couldn't figure out what happened that night, he could well end up in jail for a crime he didn't commit. She just couldn't let that happen.

11

Arriving home a few minutes later, Clara was relieved to hear nothing but silence as she let herself in the house. It seemed that Tatters had accepted his banishment to the utility room at night and had settled down in there. She resisted the temptation to open the door and take a look. Much as she would have loved to see him, disturbing him would only unsettle him and probably wake up her mother. She wasn't in the mood to deal with Jessie's complaints tonight.

After switching on the kitchen TV, she poured a mug of coffee and sat down at the table to watch the news. To her relief, no mention was made of Frank Tomeski's murder. Apparently it was now old news, and the dismal state of the economy and its effect on the town had taken its place.

Carson Dexter's stern face once more filled the screen. He complained bitterly about the lack of tourists and urged everyone to do their part to help bring more visitors to Finn's Harbor. "We need everyone to get involved," he declared, shaking his fist at the camera. "We need to put our little town on the map. Get on the social websites, tell everyone what a gorgeous, friendly, entertaining town we live in, and describe everything we have to offer. We are proud of our community and rightly so, and we need to tell the world!"

Clara rolled her eyes at the TV and stabbed the off button on the remote. Yawning, she rinsed her cup in the sink and dropped it in the dishwasher. A good night's sleep, that's what she needed, and with Tatters in the utility room, maybe tonight she'd get one.

Quietly she tiptoed down the hallway and opened her bedroom door. A low *Woof!* greeted her. Turning on the light, she saw Tatters sprawled on her bed, his tail thumping the pillow.

Clara muttered a word her mother would not approve of as she closed the door. Crossing the room to the bed, she whispered, "You're supposed to be in the utility room."

Tatters rolled over onto his back and waved his legs in the air.

Clara groaned, then got undressed, her hopes for a restful night disappearing. Settling down as best she could with a big hairy head on the pillow next to her, she drew the covers over her shoulders and closed her eyes. Almost immediately the tingling sensation began to creep over her. A vision slowly formed in her mind, shadowy at first, like a gray fog being swirled around by the wind. As the shadows disappeared she saw a black Suburban careening across a dark parking lot, narrowly missing a streetlamp as it charged out onto the road. Tires squealing, it spun around in a sharp turn and disappeared into the night.

Catching her breath, Clara sat up and switched on the bedside lamp. She had no doubt in her mind that it was the SUV Buzz had mentioned, something she had forgotten about until now. She'd dismissed it at the time, thinking it unimportant. Apparently the Sense was telling her otherwise.

She lay back down, wishing she could have seen the license plate. Had the vehicle belonged to the killer? If so, it would be tough to track down. There had to be dozens of black Suburbans driving around Finn's Harbor. Worse, if the killer was from out of town, he or she had probably left by now.

Clara frowned, wondering if there was a way she could find out if Stella Wilkins owned a black Suburban. Maybe she should talk to the motel manager again. He might have seen the car Stella was driving. Or maybe someone at the tavern saw her getting in or out of her car.

Not that she wanted to go back to the Laurel Street Tavern. In fact, the thought of a second visit turned her stomach.

She drew the covers up to her ears and tried to ignore Tatters' snoring.

To her surprise, she slept fairly well, all things considered, and woke up to hear her mother moving around in the kitchen. Tatters was awake, staring at her with expectant eyes. "I suppose you need to go outside," she said, sitting up.

Tatters leapt from the bed and padded over to the door. Sighing, Clara pulled on a robe and opened the door for him. At least this morning, she told herself, she had time to take him for a walk.

Her mother had just sat down with a bowl of cereal when Clara wandered into the kitchen. "You were late last night," she said, her tone mildly disapproving.

Clara wondered what her mother would say if she knew her daughter had spent the evening at the Laurel Street Tavern. "I didn't get there until eight thirty," she said, slipping two slices of bread into the toaster. She frowned at her mother. "You left Tatters in my room last night."

Jessie rolled her eyes. "I tried leaving him in the utility room. He howled like a banshee. I was afraid the neighbors would complain, so I shoved him into your room. He settled down right away."

"Well, why wouldn't he?" Clara poured a mug of coffee. "He had a nice, soft, cozy queen-size bed to sleep on. Incidentally, he takes up most of the room and hogs all of the covers. Not to mention his snoring."

Jessie gave her a condescending smile. "I told you it was a mistake bringing that animal home here."

Instantly regretting her lapse, Clara sought to change the subject. "I saw the mayor on TV again last night. He's worried about the lack of tourists in town. Have you noticed there's less people here than usual this summer?"

Jessie shook her head. "If you ask me, Carson Dexter is grabbing every chance he can to put his face on the television screen. He wants to be as visible as possible. I think he's planning to announce he's running for governor in the next election. He's ambitious, our mayor. He won't stop until he has a seat in the Senate."

Clara munched on a piece of toast. "Would you vote for him?"

Jessie shrugged. "I guess it would depend on who else is running. I've got nothing against Carson. He's a good mayor, and I think he's genuinely fond of the town. Of course, it's his wife's hometown, so he has to be loyal to it. If it wasn't for his wife, he wouldn't be where he is today. It's her money that's paying for his ambitions."

"Then he's lucky to have her." Clara reached for her coffee. "Personally I think he's just a tad too aggressive. He's going to bulldoze through everything and heaven help anyone who gets in his way."

Jessie smiled. "You just described the average politician."

Clara got up and took her plate and mug to the sink. "Well, I don't have much time for politicians, period."

"You're just prejudiced because Carson wants Rick Sanders arrested for murder."

"Maybe." Clara rinsed her mug and put it in the dishwasher. "But I can't respect anyone who uses his authority to ruin an innocent person's reputation."

"He's not the only one who thinks Rick is guilty." Jessie got up from the table and joined her at the sink. "Dan only let Rick go because he didn't have enough evidence to hold him."

Clara turned on her. "That's because there *is* no evidence against him. I keep telling you, Rick didn't kill that man."

"Then why was the body found in Rick's truck?"

"Anyone could have put it there."

"Why? Why not just leave the body lying on the ground?"

"I don't know. I don't know any of the answers. I wish I did. I just know that Rick is innocent."

Jessie's face softened. "All right, honey. Just don't let your personal feelings get in the way of your common sense, okay?"

"Don't worry. I won't." Clara dried her hands on a paper towel, squashing the urge to tell her mother that the Quinn Sense had convinced her of Rick's innocence. She had kept her secret for so long, hoping that by doing so she could ignore its presence and perhaps get rid of it altogether. Instead she had spent most of her life fighting it when it was there and cursing it when it wasn't.

Still, there was always the hope that it would help her find some of the answers she needed, and as long as the Sense was working for her and not against her, she welcomed its contribution. Right now, it was noticeably absent, and she decided that a brisk walk with Tatters might help clear her mind.

Tatters showed his excitement by dragging her down the driveway, until she dug in her heels and ordered him to "Stay!"

He paused, looking back at her with an expression that clearly said, *Are you kidding me?*

"I'm in charge of this walk," Clara told him as she started down the street, holding him back on a short leash. "So, either you do exactly what I tell you, or we go straight back home and you can spend the rest of the day in the utility room."

Tatters glanced back at her over his shoulder and trotted obediently a few paces in front of her.

She was so busy watching the dog she failed to notice the red Ferrari pulling up at the curb ahead of her. It wasn't until the stocky figure of the mayor climbed out and patted Tatters on the head that she realized he had intentionally stopped to speak to her.

Dazzled by the magnificence of the sports car, she hauled the dog closer.

"Good morning." Carson Dexter bowed his head in an old-fashioned greeting. "Lovely morning for a walk."

Clara glanced up at the clouded sky. "Er . . . yes, it is."

Carson smiled. "I take it you know who I am?"

Clara nodded.

"In that case, I'm sure you'll take it seriously when I advise you to quit interfering in police business. Poking around in matters that don't concern you is not only unwarranted, it could also be considered an obstruction of justice. I'm sure you wouldn't want to find yourself facing a judge in court. Have a nice day."

Clara watched him climb back into the Ferrari and roar down the street, her mind still entranced by the car. As it turned the corner and disappeared, however, the mayor's words hit her like a brick.

Had he really just threatened to take her to court for simply asking questions? How had he known? Had someone complained to him about her? Could it have possibly been Frank Tomeski's murderer, afraid she was getting too close?

Shaken, she continued on her walk, her resolve growing with every step. No one, not even the mayor of Finn's Harbor, was going to stop her investigation. Somehow, she would have to find out who told him she'd been asking questions.

One thing was for certain. She wouldn't vote for Carson Dexter for governor, even if he were running against a gorilla.

She was still fuming when she left the house for the bookstore, after settling Tatters down in her room with the radio on and a bone to chew.

Molly and Stephanie were both serving customers when Clara arrived at the Raven's Nest. She'd meant to get there early so she would have enough time to pay a visit to the hardware store. Given the mood she was in, however, it was just as well she'd left too late to talk to Rick.

She stashed her purse behind the counter and quickly

checked the morning's receipts. It looked as if the Raven's Nest had been busy. She was about to join her cousin in the aisles when she heard the *ping* of the doorbell. Looking up, her stomach took a nosedive when she saw the chief of police.

Dan Petersen was a jovial-looking man, especially when dressed as casually as he was now, though his ice blue eyes could freeze someone into silence with one glance. He ran a tight police force and was respected by the vast majority of the community. There wasn't much that got past Dan, and Clara was well aware of his perceptive abilities as he halted in front of her, his mouth tilted in a half smile.

"How's the bookselling business?"

"Pretty good." Clara waved a hand at the aisles. "The fantasy books are doing real well. It's a popular genre right now."

"Ah." Dan nodded, his hands behind his back. "Vampires and all that stuff."

"Some of it, yes." Clara tilted her head to one side. "Did you want to look at some?"

"Vampires?" Dan gave a mock shudder. "No, thanks." He looked around. "I did want a word or two with you and your cousin. Is she around?"

Clara glanced nervously down an aisle. "She's serving a customer at the moment." She frowned. "Is something wrong?"

Dan pursed his lips. "Depends on how you look at things. I heard you two have been bugging people about the bowling alley murder."

"Bugging?" Clara shook her head. "I wouldn't say we were bugging people. Just asking a few questions, that's all."

Dan rocked back on his heels. "You know that's my job, don't you?"

Clara uttered a shaky laugh. "We're not trying to be cops. We were just curious."

"Curious? Hmm." Dan studied her, making her more uncomfortable as the seconds ticked by. Finally, he added, "I know you were a great help in solving Ana Jordan's murder last year, but I hope you're not getting the idea you can do better than the police. You were lucky you weren't badly hurt, you know."

Clara gave him a weak smile.

"The mayor thinks you're taking all this a little too seriously. We're doing our best to solve this case, and we're making headway. It might be a good idea to leave the investigating to us."

Clare stared at him. "You found the murderer?"

"Not yet." Dan turned toward the door. "But we will." He paused and looked back at her. "Watch your step, both of you. Murder is a dangerous business." With that, he opened the door and disappeared into the street.

Clara let out her breath just as Stephanie emerged from the aisle, followed by an elderly woman who muttered something under her breath.

Stephanie rolled her eyes at Clara and hurried over to the counter. "Yes, Mrs. Riley, I know books are expensive, but they give us so much pleasure, they're worth every penny."

"I don't know how I can afford to read anymore," the woman grumbled, handing over a credit card. "Everything's going up, except my pension."

Stephanie rang up the purchase and gave the card back to the woman. "Thank you, Mrs. Riley. It was good to see you again. I hope you enjoy the books."

Mrs. Riley took the bag Stephanie handed her and headed for the door, nodding at Clara as she passed. "They help keep my mind off things," she said as Clara opened the door for her. "I don't watch the news anymore. Too many terrible things going on. It scares me to death." She nodded at the hardware store. "I don't know how you young women can work here with a murderer just across the street."

Clara was about to open her mouth and tell the old bat how wrong she was when she caught sight of Stephanie frantically shaking her head. She closed her mouth again and gave the woman a tight smile. Waiting until the door closed behind Mrs. Riley, she let out her breath in an explosive, "Ignorant old woman!"

Stephanie rushed over to her. "I'm glad you didn't say anything to her. You know how she gossips all over town. I didn't want her telling everyone we're trying to solve the case and tip off the killer."

"It's too late," Clara said, running her fingers through her bangs. "According to Dan and our esteemed mayor, news of our investigation is all over town."

Stephanie's jaw dropped. "How do you know?"

"Carson Dexter came to my house this morning and stopped me on the street. He warned me we could be charged with obstruction of justice and interfering in police business."

"That's ridiculous." Stephanie looked over her shoulder as if worried who might overhear. "What did Dan say?"

"He strongly suggested we leave the investigating to him."

"Crap. We'd better hold off on asking questions, then."

"It doesn't matter." Clara wandered over to the counter. "We don't have anyone else to ask."

"We need to sit down and talk about what we know so far. Maybe something we haven't thought about will pop up."

"I did have a vision last night, about the SUV Buzz mentioned."

Stephanie joined her behind the counter. "Really? What did you see?

"Not much. I don't know if there's a connection there or not."

"We definitely need to talk. How about coming over my house for dinner tonight?"

Clara shook her head. "Can't. I've left Tatters with my mother for the last two nights. I have to be there this evening."

"All right, I'll call you. We can talk on the phone." Stephanie glanced at the clock. "It's time for me to leave. We'll talk tonight." She grabbed up her purse and patted

Clara's arm. "Don't worry. We'll get to the bottom of all this somehow."

Clara watched her go, wishing she could believe that. Right now it all seemed so hopeless. Maybe she'd been naïve, thinking that just because she'd solved one murder she could do so again. *Where are you, Quinn Sense? Give me just one tiny clue. Anything.*

No voices answered her, and she walked back to the aisles. Maybe Stephanie was right. Maybe something they'd missed would occur to them when they talked. Feeling a little less dejected, she approached a customer and offered her help.

She arrived home that evening to find her mother deep into a book and Tatters lying in front of the TV. The dog raised his head when she walked into the living room. Getting up to greet her, his tail narrowly missed the lamp sitting on the end table.

Clara fondled his ears and shook her head at her mother. "How can you read with the TV blaring like that?"

Jessie shrugged and put the book down. "I shut it out."

"Why don't you just turn it off?"

"Tatters likes to watch." Seeing Clara grin, she picked up the book again. "Besides, you know I like sound in the house when I'm alone." She turned a page and adjusted her reading glasses. "There's lasagna in the oven. You just have to warm it up."

Thanking her, Clara crossed to the kitchen and turned on the stove. The newspaper lay on the table and she picked it up. She had to turn three pages before she found what she was looking for—a short paragraph on the local page.

There are no new developments in the bowling alley murder case. Police are still investigating, and Rick Sanders, owner of Parson's Hardware, is still considered a person of interest in the case. Mayor Carson Dexter continues to urge all residents of Finn's Harbor to come forward with any information that may be helpful. You may contact the police or the mayor at City Hall.

Clara dropped the newspaper on the table and opened up a cupboard. Grabbing a plate off the shelf, she was about to carry it over to the stove when a voice spoke distinctly in her ear. *City Hall. City Hall. City Hall.*

Frowning, Clara stood quite still in the middle of the kitchen. *What about City Hall?*

The voice refused to answer. Frustrated, she walked back into the living room.

Her mother looked up as Clara headed for the hallway. "Are you all right? You look as if you're ready to punch someone in the face."

Clara made herself smile. "Just tired. I have some stuff to do on my computer. I'll come back and eat in a little while."

Jessie nodded. "Just don't let the lasagna burn."

"I won't." She walked down the hall, with Tatters padding behind her. He followed her into her room and jumped up on her bed, where he curled up with his nose in his tail. His gaze followed her as she walked over to her desk and sat down.

"We'll go out later," she promised him. "Right after I've eaten." Nudging on her computer, she stared at the monitor, waiting for it to boot up. *City Hall.* What the heck was the Sense trying to tell her? To go see Dan? Maybe tell him everything she knew? But she didn't know anything that would help. Except the name of Frank Tomeski's girlfriend and the police might already have that information. Was that what the Sense was trying to tell her? That Stella Wilkins had killed her boyfriend in a fit of jealous rage?

Logging on to the Internet, she hoped she'd at least get to eat before her cousin called. A quick glance at her e-mails showed nothing interesting, and she leaned back in her chair. She needed to balance her checkbook but couldn't seem to drum up enough enthusiasm to do it. Instead, she pulled up the website for the *Chronicle.* Sure enough, there it was: the same paragraph that she'd seen in the newspaper. This time, however, no voice echoed the words *City Hall.*

An idea struck her, and she scrolled up to the search engine and entered the name *Frank Tomeski.* After skimming through a couple of paragraphs that seemed to have nothing to do with the murdered man, a headline caught her eye: *YOUNG GIRL FOUND DEAD IN PORTLAND APARTMENT.* Curious, she read on. The article described the scene where a young woman, Amy Tomeski, was found dead from an overdose of prescription drugs. The police found a suicide note, and the medical examiner reported that the woman had been pregnant. The baby did not survive.

Clara's first thought was how sad that a young mother had been so desperate she'd taken her own life and that of her unborn baby. Her next thought was even more disturbing. Could this woman possibly have been a relative of Frank Tomeski?

She skimmed the rest of the page but could find nothing more. She tried to sort out her thoughts, but her mind seemed to be blank, and she raised her chin and stared at the ceiling. "Darn you, Quinn Sense. Where the heck are you when I need you?"

She hadn't realized she'd spoken out loud until Tatters whined. She looked at him and he sat up, staring at her with anxious brown eyes. "It's okay, boy," she said softly.

He whined again in answer and jumped off the bed. She held out her hand, and he trotted over to her, where he nudged her hand with his cold nose.

"It's okay," she said again. "Let's go eat."

She got up and he followed close on her heels as she walked down the hallway to the living room. Her mother was still engrossed in her book and didn't look up when Clara told her, "I'm going to eat. Do you want anything?"

Her mother simply waved a hand and went on reading.

After sharing some of the lasagna with Tatters, Clara stuffed the dishes in the dishwasher and had just finished when her cell phone rang. Stephanie's voice greeted her, and aware of Jessie listening in the living room, Clara answered quietly, "I'll call you back in a minute."

Her mother looked up when she walked back into the living room. "I suppose that was that hardware man calling you."

Clara bit back a sharp response. "Nope," she said carefully, "it was Stephanie."

"Oh." Her mother gave her an odd look. "Well, I don't know why you can't just talk to her with me here." She squinted at her. "You're not in trouble, are you?"

Clara smiled. "Not as far as I know."

"Good. You'd tell me if you were, right?"

"Of course." Clara headed for the hallway.

"I'm going to bed," Jessie announced. "Do you want me to turn off the TV?"

Clara nodded. "I'm taking Tatters for a walk in a little while, and then I'm going to bed, too."

"Glad to hear it. You stay up way too late in my opinion." Jessie switched off the TV and got up. "You'll be old before your time if you don't get your rest."

"Yes, Mother." Clara continued down the hallway.

"And don't let that dog sleep on your bed again. It's not good for either of you."

"Yes, Mother. Good-night!" Thankfully she closed the bedroom door, and Tatters jumped gleefully on the bed and settled down.

Clara pulled out her chair and sat down in front of the

computer. Opening her cell phone, she stabbed out her cousin's number and waited for her to answer.

Stephanie's voice was muted when she spoke. "George has gone to bed," she said. "I think he's coming down with a cold."

"Oh, I'm sorry."

"So am I. He can be such a baby when he's sick." Clara heard the sound of ice clinking in a glass, then Stephanie added, "I just made him some iced tea. I can't talk long."

"It's okay. I can't, either. My mother is beginning to wonder what all the secrecy is about."

"You didn't tell her, did you?"

Clara rolled her eyes at the alarm in her cousin's voice. "No, of course not. Though it's only a matter of time before she finds out."

"I remember how freaked out she got the last time we did this."

"Well, hopefully she won't find out until it's all over."

"What's all over? We still don't have any idea who did this."

Clara leaned back on her chair. "No, we don't. Though I did find out something interesting on the computer tonight." She recited as much of the article about Amy Tomeski as she could remember.

"Oh, that poor woman," Stephanie said when she was done. "She must have been in a terrible state to do that. Can you imagine thinking that you and your baby would be better off dead?"

She sounded close to tears, and Clara hurried on. "The thing is, she could be related to Frank Tomeski."

There was a long pause while Stephanie thought about it. "That's quite a long shot."

"I know, but it's not a very common name. I looked it up in the white pages for Portland. It's not even listed in there."

"Even if she was related, what would that have to do with Frank Tomeski's murder?"

"I don't know." Clara frowned. "I just have a gut feeling about it.

Stephanie's voice rose a notch. "The Quinn Sense?"

"Maybe. It told me I need to go to City Hall. I think we need to talk to Dan about this."

"But none of it makes sense. When did this Amy person die?"

"According to the article, about five years ago."

"I just don't see how something that happened that long ago could have anything to do with the murder."

Clara was inclined to agree, yet she couldn't rid herself of the niggling feeling that she was onto something. "I think we need to find out for sure before we go to Dan."

"How do we do that?"

"By talking with the one person we know who knew Frank Tomeski."

"Buzz Lamont?" Stephanie's voice rose another notch. "Are you sure you want to talk to him again?"

"No, but I don't know what else to do."

After another long pause, Stephanie's sigh echoed down the line. "All right. When?"

"I'll let you know." She hung up, certain she was on the right track. Something was telling her that the key to the puzzle lay with Amy Tomeski's death. Her last hope was that Buzz Lamont would be able to explain why.

After making a couple of calls the next morning and walking Tatters, Clara left the house early. She wasn't too excited about talking to Buzz Lamont on her own, but having given it some thought, she'd decided if she was going to go against the wishes of the mayor and the chief of police, it was better she didn't involve Stephanie this time. She'd fill her cousin in afterward on what she'd learned, if anything.

She was told at the landscaper's office that Buzz was working at an insurance office. To her relief he was in full view of the street. He didn't seem too happy to see her when she approached him. In fact, he turned his back on her and attacked the flower bed with his rake as if he were trying to kill everything in it.

She edged her way around him and spoke his name. "I'm sorry to bug you again, but I really need your help."

He looked up at her, his leathery face set in a frown. "I'm busy."

With a sinking feeling in her stomach, she tried again. "Please? It's desperately important."

"So is my job." He glanced over his shoulder. "And my family. If someone sees me talking to you . . ."

"I'll be really quick. I just need to know if Frank Tomeski was related to a young woman named Amy Tomeski."

Buzz kept his head down, but she could tell by the sudden jerk of his shoulders that she'd hit a nerve. When he didn't answer, she added softly, "Who was she?"

She had almost given up when Buzz muttered, "Amy was Frank's sister. She killed herself when some guy got her pregnant and then left town."

"Do you know who the father of her baby was?"

"No, I don't." Buzz turned on her so fiercely she stepped back a couple of paces. He followed her, drawing closer to speak in a low voice. "Listen, lady. I don't know anything about Frank's murder, and I don't want to know. If you want my advice, you'll drop it and quit asking questions before someone decides you're getting too nosy."

Every instinct urged Clara to do just that, but she had come this far, she wasn't about to give up now. "Like who?"

Buzz looked as if he were about to explode. He took a deep breath, then let it out through his clenched teeth. "If I tell you something, will you swear to me you'll never let on where you heard it?"

Hope rising, she crossed her hand over her chest. "I swear."

Buzz looked around, then drew even closer. "About a month ago, I sent Frank an e-mail. I thought I recognized someone his sister used to work with, back in Portland. I sent Frank a pic and asked him if it was the same guy. Frank never answered me, and I figured he never got the e-mail."

Clara felt a stab of excitement. "Who was the guy? Do you know his name?"

Buzz twisted his mouth in a wry smile. "Everyone knows his name." He looked over his shoulder again, then added in a low whisper, "It's Carson Dexter."

12

Clara arrived at the bookstore just in time to catch Stephanie as she was leaving. Surprised to see her cousin there on her day off, she shook her head. "Just can't stay away, huh?"

Stephanie shrugged. "I had to come in to pick up some bills." She glanced at the clock. "You're late. Did you oversleep?"

"No, I was talking to someone." Clara answered Molly's wave with a flap of her hand. "I need to talk to you." She glanced over her shoulder. "Privately."

Stephanie looked worried. "There are customers in the Nook, and we're pretty busy right now. Can it wait?"

Clara hesitated, then reluctantly nodded. "When?"

Stephanie frowned. "I've got the kids the rest of the day. George won't be home until late tonight. He's going to a meeting. Why don't you come by the house on your way home tonight? I'll fix you something to eat."

Clara sighed, thinking of Tatters having to put up with her mother again. "Okay. I'll see you then."

Stephanie gave her an anxious look. "Is it important? You're not in trouble, are you?"

"Why does everyone automatically think I'm in trouble?"

Stephanie lowered her voice. "We *are* investigating a murder, remember?"

"How can I forget?"

"Is it about the murder?"

"I think so." Clara smiled at the customer heading toward her. "We'll talk tonight. Go get your kids."

Stephanie looked as if she wanted to hear more, but Clara was already greeting the elderly man, and after a moment's hesitation, Stephanie rushed out the door.

It was late afternoon before Clara had a chance to call her mother. "Not *again*," Jessie said when Clara told her she was having dinner with Stephanie. "Ever since you brought that dog home you've been gone more than you're here."

"Then it's a good thing you have Tatters for company," Clara said, hoping Jessie wouldn't cause too much of a fuss. "Why don't you take him for a walk? He'd love it, and it would do you good."

"I'm on my feet all day at the library. I don't need to be dragged all over town by an unruly animal."

"You know that Tatters is perfectly behaved when he's with you," Clara said, crossing her fingers.

"Oh, very well. But we can't go on like this. I have a life too, you know. I can't spend all my time staying home to look after a dog."

"Then just leave Tatters in my room. He'll be fine until I get home."

"He gets lonely on his own." Jessie's voice softened to a low crooning. "Don't you, my sweet? Yes, he's *such* a good boy."

Clara grinned. "Okay, then. I won't be late." She hung up, satisfied that Tatters was in excellent hands.

She returned to the counter just as the door opened and Rick strolled in. Delighted to see him, she sang out a greeting.

"Hi, yourself." He grinned at her and walked over to the cookbook table. "Got anything new on here?"

She hurried to join him, her anxious gaze taking in his face. He looked tired, as if he hadn't been sleeping well. "You okay?" she asked, and got a nod for an answer.

"I don't think I saw this one the other day. Is it new?" He picked up a book and started flipping pages.

"That one came in about a month ago." She picked up another book with pictures of fruit all over the jacket. "This is the latest one to come in, but I think you've seen this one, too."

He took it from her and opened it. "Yeah, I did see it."

He put the book down. "I had a visitor today. The mayor of Finn's Harbor stopped by."

Her stomach flipped over. "What did he want?"

"I'm not sure. He kind of wandered around the store for a while, then asked me if I'd seen Dan lately."

"What did you tell him?"

"I told him I hadn't talked to Dan in the last couple of days." Rick frowned. "I think he was trying to find out if I'm still a murder suspect. He's not going to give up until I'm in jail."

"That's never going to happen."

She'd sounded so adamant, he raised his eyebrows. "Do you know something I don't?"

She caught herself before she could blurt out anything that would tip him off to her recent activities. "I just know that you didn't do it."

His smile looked a little fragile. "Thanks. I needed that."

"It's true." How she wished she could give him something to hang on to—some small ray of hope that all this would be over before much longer. She was still so unsure about what she did know, and what it all meant.

Buzz's revelation about Carson Dexter had seemed so significant when she'd first heard it. Now that she'd had time to think about it, however, she wasn't at all sure that the mayor's connection to Frank Tomeski's sister had anything to do with his murder. Even if it did, how could they convince Dan of that, much less prove anything?

She could only hope that talking it over with Stephanie

would help her unravel the tangle of thoughts in her mind and enable her to think more clearly. Right now, the more she tried to sort out what she knew, the more confused she got. And that wasn't helping Rick at all.

———

Stephanie greeted Clara with an anxious face when she arrived at her house that evening. "The kids are playing outside," she said, leading Clara into the dining room. "They've already eaten, so we can have dinner in peace."

Glancing at the large chicken Caesar salad waiting for her, Clara grinned in appreciation. "That looks terrific."

"Good. I opened a bottle of wine. Help yourself while I get it." She returned a moment later with a bottle of pinot gris and filled her cousin's wineglass. "Here." She pushed the glass closer to Clara's plate. "You look like you can use this."

Clara picked up the glass. "Here's to solving the murder."

"Amen." Stephanie filled her own glass and took a hefty sip. "Mmm, that's a good one." She sat down opposite her cousin. "So, what's up? Have you found out anything else about the case?"

Clara waited until she'd swallowed another sip of wine before answering. "I talked to Buzz Lamont this morning."

"You didn't!" Stephanie's eyes were wide with horror. "By yourself? Why didn't you wait for me to go with you? That was stupid."

Clara shrugged. "It was okay. He was working close to the street."

"So what did he tell you?"

"He knew Amy Tomeski."

"He did?" Stephanie paused with her fork halfway to her mouth.

"He told me she was Frank Tomeski's sister and she used to work in Portland with someone he knows here in Finn's Harbor."

"Who is it? Anyone we know?"

Clara smiled. "Our esteemed mayor, Carson Dexter."

Stephanie's fork clattered onto her plate. "Are you kidding? If he knew Amy Tomeski, wouldn't he have known Frank, too?"

"Not necessarily. If he had, I would think he'd have identified Frank when his picture was on TV. Maybe he never met the guy."

Stephanie's eyes grew wider. "Unless he didn't want anyone to know he knew him." She paused, apparently turning things over in her mind. Her voice was hushed when she added, "You think Carson Dexter killed Frank Tomeski?"

Clara let out her breath in a rush. "I don't know what I think right now. All I know is that the mayor knew Amy Tomeski. That connects him to the victim of a murder."

"That doesn't mean he killed him."

"No, but it does add him to our list of suspects."

Stephanie met her gaze. "You're not suggesting that you question him?"

"You don't think it's a good idea?"

"No, I don't. Even if he is guilty, and it's a big if, I doubt very much that he'd answer your questions. You could be in a lot of trouble after he warned you to butt out."

Clara shook her head. "I guess. I just don't know where to go from here."

Stephanie picked up her wineglass again. "You need to conjure up the Sense."

"I wish I could." Clara dug her fork into her salad. "It really hasn't been much help lately. Though it did say that one thing right before I found out about Amy."

"What was that again?"

"It said *City Hall.*"

Stephanie choked on her wine. "Do you think it was telling you the mayor was a suspect?"

"I don't know. There a lot of people who work in City Hall." She paused, trying to grab hold of something niggling in the back of her mind. "Wait, I just remembered. The day of the murder, Rick was in the bookstore chasing after Tatters."

Stephanie grinned. "Yeah, I remember you telling me. The dog was running after Roberta. I didn't think anyone could get the better of that woman, much less a dog."

Clara smiled at the memory. "She was really scared of him. If she knew what a sweetheart he is, she'd feel pretty silly about the whole thing."

"Nah, she'd insist he's a killer dog just to save face."

"Yes, well, anyway, I remember Rick coming in, pretty steamed at Tatters because he had to leave customers alone in his store. He said one of them was asking where to find City Hall."

Stephanie picked up a roll and broke it in half. "I'm not following."

"Frank Tomeski was in the store that day." Clara shook her head as Stephanie offered her half the roll. "What if it was Frank asking where to find City Hall? What if he was looking for the mayor?"

Stephanie dropped the piece of roll onto her plate. "Or what if he was looking for the police because he was afraid someone was out to kill him?"

"But he didn't go to the police. Dan didn't know who he was until the motel manager identified him two days later."

"Maybe he never got there because the killer found him first."

Clara put down her fork and leaned back on her chair. "You're making things even more confusing."

"I'm sorry." Stephanie lifted her own fork and pointed it at her cousin. "I just think you should be sure about everything before you go accusing the mayor of murder. Even Dan isn't going to listen to that. He and Carson Dexter are best buddies."

"I know that." Clara gazed miserably at her plate. "I just wish I knew what to do."

Stephanie's frown softened. "We'll think of something. Why don't you try to find out more about the mayor's connection to Amy Tomeski? You're so good at researching stuff on the computer. Something might turn up that will help make sense of all this."

Clara sighed. "I guess you're right. I need to think about it some more and maybe the Sense will come through for me. Though I'm not going to hold my breath for that." She finished her salad, only half listening as Stephanie prattled on about her kids and their latest escapades.

"They remind me so much of us when we were that age," she said as Clara helped her carry dishes to the kitchen.

Clara opened the dishwasher and started stacking dishes. "Do you remember the time we decided to sell some stuff so we could get roller skates?"

"How could I forget? We were grounded for weeks after that."

"Yeah, well, I don't think your mom was too happy when she found out you sold her pearls for two dollars."

Stephanie smiled. "Good thing it was Katie Minsen who bought them. Her mom made her give them back."

"After she'd cut them up to fit her dolls."

"I know. I lost a month's allowance to pay for them to be restrung." Stephanie reached for a paper towel and wiped the counter. "It wasn't just me. You tried to sell your dad's golf clubs." She laughed. "I can still see his face when he came tearing across the lawn to rescue them before someone snapped them up."

Clara started to laugh with her, then choked as tears unexpectedly filled her eyes.

Stephanie dropped the towel and threw an arm around her. "Oh, I'm sorry, Clara. I wasn't thinking."

"It's okay." Feeling foolish, Clara swiped at her eyes with the back of her hand. "I just miss him. He's been gone three years now, and it still hits me now and then. I guess I'm feeling down over this darn murder thing. No matter how we try, we can't seem to get any closer to solving it, and it doesn't look as if Dan is having any better luck and Rick—"

She broke off with a laugh. "Listen to me. I'm whining like I used to whenever you got me into trouble."

"*I* got *you* into trouble?" Stephanie drew back, her face pink with indignation. "You didn't seem to have any problem going along with everything. Until we got caught, and then it was always *my* fault!"

Clara shrugged. "You were always the one with the brilliant ideas. Ideas, I might add, that usually backfired on us."

Stephanie looked about to explode, then her face broke into a grin. "We had fun, though, didn't we?"

Clara grinned back and reached out to hug her. "We sure did. And now I'd better get home and see what kind of fun my mother is having with Tatters."

Arriving home a few minutes later, she was relieved to see her mother dozing in front of the TV. Tatters got up as usual as Clara walked into the living room and ran over to greet her, waking her mother up in the process.

"Oh, there you are," Jessie said, sitting up. "What time is it?"

"Not yet ten." Clara peered at her. "Are you okay?"

"What?" Jessie frowned, then added with a yawn, "Of

course I'm all right. Just tired. This ridiculous dog wore me out on the beach."

Tatters' ears pricked up, and he looked at Clara with pleading eyes.

"Look at him," Jessie said, sounding disgusted. "He's been romping on the sand for over an hour and he's still not satisfied."

"I'll take him out later." Clara started for the hallway.

"So, how was dinner?"

Clara paused, knowing she would have to submit to an interrogation before she could escape to her room.

Ten minutes later, after she'd avoided the awkward questions and answered the less incriminating ones, she seated herself in front of her computer.

Stephanie had been right: it took her only a few minutes to track down some more information. Going back to the article about Amy Tomeski, she discovered that the young woman had worked for an investment company in Portland. After finding the company's website, Clara found an article that mentioned Carson Dexter.

Apparently the mayor had worked for the company for many years, and had met his wife, Melinda Wingate, after his promotion to general manager. Melinda was the daughter of a wealthy business tycoon, and several years after their marriage the couple left Portland and moved back to Finn's Harbor, where Melinda had spent most of her childhood. There they bought a sumptuous home, and Carson served on the city council until he was elected mayor.

Clara stared at the words on the screen. It was all very

interesting, but she didn't really see how any of it connected to Frank Tomeski's murder.

Without warning the familiar sensation swept over her. She tensed, waiting for the voice to tell her what she needed to know. *Time. It's all a matter of time.*

She sat up, frowning in frustration. "What the heck does that mean?"

Lying on the bed, Tatters raised his head and whined.

"It's okay, boy. We'll go in a minute."

The dog lowered his nose to his paws and kept his gaze on her.

Ignoring him, Clara gazed at the article again. As she did so, the words on the screen faded, to be replaced by a scene of a darkened parking lot. Two men struggling in the shadows. One dragging the other across the ground. Then a black SUV careening across the parking spaces and narrowly missing the fence as it plunged into the street.

Clara blinked and found herself once more staring at the words of the article. If only she'd been able to see the faces of the men. Or even the license plate of the SUV.

The memory of the mayor stepping out of a red Ferrari snapped into her mind. Was the Sense trying to tell her she was on the wrong track? Then what was all that about it being a matter of time?

Losing patience, she clicked off-line and stood up. Tatters was at the door before she'd taken a step. "Okay, boy." She opened the door, and he shot down the hallway. He halted at the front door and stood looking at her, ears back and tail wagging furiously.

"Wait a minute," she told him. "I have to get your leash."

The light was still on in the living room, though the TV had been turned off. Jessie was in the kitchen, rinsing out the coffeepot. She looked up as Clara walked in. "Oh, I thought you'd gone to bed."

"No, I'm going to take the dog for a walk first." Clara glanced around the kitchen. "Where's the leash?"

"I left it on the TV. The news was on when I came in from taking the dog for a walk. Carson Dexter was on there, still complaining about Dan and his police department. He's not happy that there's been no arrest in the murder case."

Clara grunted in reply.

Jessie frowned at her. "Still convinced that your hardware man didn't do it?"

"He's not my hardware man, and yes, I'm still convinced. What's more, I think it's disgusting the way the mayor rolls around town, accusing innocent people without any justification whatsoever. I know what I'd like to do with his red Ferrari."

Jessie raised her eyebrows. "My, we are belligerent tonight. What has Carson done to upset you?"

"Nothing, except try to put an innocent man in jail." Clara headed out into the living room.

Jessie followed her. "By the way, that red Ferrari

doesn't belong to Carson. It's his wife's car. He borrows it now and then when she's out of town. I've often wondered if she knows he's driving it. According to what I hear, she's terribly possessive about her belongings."

Clara stopped short. "If it's not the mayor's car, then what does he drive?"

She really didn't need to hear the answer. She already knew.

"Oh, haven't you seen him driving around in it?" Jessie picked up the dog's leash and handed it to her. "Carson drives a black Suburban."

———

Clara had walked all the way down to the harbor before the message sent by the Quinn Sense became clear. She could hardly wait to get back to the house, and poor Tatters had his walk cut short as she hurried back to her computer.

She read the articles again carefully and checked the dates they were written. Then she pulled up the website of the *Harbor Chronicle*. It took a while but she eventually found what she was looking for: an article about Melinda Wingate Dexter returning to her hometown and buying back the family mansion that her father had sold years earlier.

Carson had told the reporter that he had suggested the move back to his wife's hometown because of their concerns about a healthy environment for their children. The air was so much cleaner in Finn's Harbor, Carson had maintained, and the lifestyle so much more beneficial to their well-being.

Once more Clara checked the dates, then sat back on her chair, heart thumping. Amy Tomeski had killed herself one week after Carson Dexter had left town. Buzz Lamont had e-mailed Frank Tomeski after recognizing the mayor as having worked at the same company where Amy had worked.

Could it be that Carson was the father of Amy's unborn baby? Had Frank found out where Carson was, five years after Amy's death, and come to Finn's Harbor seeking revenge? Could Carson Dexter have killed Frank in self-defense? If so, why hadn't he simply gone to Dan and explained everything?

The memory of words spoken by Buzz Lamont clicked into her mind. *I've got a good job, and a wife and family. If news got out about my past, I could kiss all that good-bye.*

Of course. Carson Dexter would probably lose everything, including his ambitions for the governor's office and the Senate, if his wife and the residents of Finn's Harbor found out he'd had an affair with Amy Tomeski.

Clara got up. She had to talk to Rick again. Maybe it wasn't too late to call him. She picked up her cell phone and began punching in numbers. Before she hit the last one, however, she snapped her phone shut.

She couldn't get his hopes up yet. Although her theory neatly linked together everything she had discovered, she still had no way of proving it. She could go to Dan with all the facts, but was it enough to convince the chief of police that his mayor, and close friend, was a murderer? It seemed highly unlikely.

She wanted to call Stephanie to test her theory, but it was getting late. It would just have to wait until tomorrow.

She slept late and awoke to the sound of her cell phone jingling. Yawning, she reached for it and snapped it open.

Stephanie's voice answered her. "Were you asleep? It's almost nine thirty."

"I was up late." Clara yawned again. "What's up? Everything okay at the store?"

"Yes, everything's fine."

"What is it, Steffie? Are you all right?" Alerted by the odd tone of her cousin's voice, Clara struggled to sit up, dislodging Tatters, who was lying on her feet. He huffed out his breath and settled down again at the bottom of the bed.

Stephanie cleared her throat. "Clara, I wanted to tell you before you heard it on the news. Rick has been arrested. They found his DNA in a bloodstain on Frank Tomeski's clothing."

Clara clutched the phone so hard her knuckles turned white. "I don't believe it. There has to be some explanation."

"I'm sorry, Clara. I know—"

"No! I won't believe it. I've got to go. I'll talk to you later." She snapped the phone shut and swung her legs off the side of the bed. Grabbing her robe, she headed for the living room. Jessie had already left for work, and the smell of coffee brewing in the kitchen drew Clara in there.

Propped up in front of her coffee mug was a note from her mother saying she was going out to dinner with a friend after work and would be home late. Clara wondered briefly if her mother was going on a date, but her worries about Rick chased away any thoughts about Jessie's love life.

She turned on the TV and poured a mug of coffee, bringing it back to the table to sit down. Scrolling through the channels, she found one showing the news, but it was national news, and after a few moments she turned it off.

The coffee burned her throat, but she kept drinking, needing the jolt of caffeine to clear her mind. Rick arrested. It didn't make sense. Why would he kill a complete stranger?

He didn't, of course. She was almost certain that Carson Dexter had killed Frank Tomeski, probably in self-defense. It would certainly explain his frantic efforts to get Rick arrested for the crime. With Rick in jail, Carson was free and clear.

How the devil was she going to prove it? She had nothing to go on, except for Buzz Lamont almost being run over by a black Suburban, and her own visions that no one in their right mind would take seriously.

Well, maybe her family, but they weren't the police, and Dan Petersen dealt in facts, not weird fantasies and whispering voices. Clara buried her face in her hands. What was she going to do? How could she save Rick from being imprisoned for something he didn't do?

No matter how hard she concentrated, no voices answered her. No visions appeared in her mind. Nothing.

Frustrated beyond belief, she picked up the newspaper that Jessie had left on the table and threw it across the room. Damn the Quinn Sense. For all it was worth, she'd be better off without it. Much better off.

13

Just as Clara reached the bookstore later that morning, Stephanie flew out the door. "I've got to get groceries," she said, "and the kids are waiting for me to pick them up. Molly's got her hands full in the Nook, and there are a couple of customers in the aisles—"

"Don't worry, I've got it." Clara opened the door. "Can you come over to my house tonight? My mother won't be home and we need to talk."

"Sure! George will be home so I can leave the kids with him." Stephanie paused to peer up at Clara's face. "Are you all right?"

Clara nodded. "Don't worry about me. Get going yourself."

Stephanie hovered a moment longer, then with a wave, dashed down the street.

Feeling a sense of impending doom, Clara walked into the bookstore.

She was busy most of the day, which was a good thing, as it helped keep her mind off her troubles. She had about an hour left to go when Roberta Prince walked into the store, pretending to be interested in a display of a best-selling fantasy novel.

Since Clara knew for a fact that Roberta didn't read fantasy, or much fiction at all come to that, it was pretty obvious that the woman was there to talk about Rick.

It didn't take long for her theory to be proven correct.

"I suppose you know Rick has been arrested," Roberta said, running a finger along the counter as if she were testing for dust. "They found his DNA on the murdered guy."

"So I heard." Clara pretended to sort through the day's receipts, hoping that Roberta would take the hint and leave.

"I guess he'll be charged with the murder."

Clara bit her lip to keep quiet.

Roberta waited for several seconds for Clara to answer, then blurted out, "I don't know what I ever saw in that man. To think I actually bought the stupid stationer's so I could be close to a murderer. I should have known. I always thought there was something creepy about him."

Clara could keep silent no longer. "You wanted to marry him," she said, striving to keep her voice low. "You didn't think he was so creepy a week ago."

Roberta shrugged. "Just goes to show you can never

tell what someone is really like. Thank God we found out before one of us did something really stupid."

"Like what?"

"Like falling in love with him or something." Roberta stalked to the door. "I always thought you might be interested in him."

"He's a good friend." Clara dropped the receipts and walked out from behind the counter. "Not that it's any of your business. I will tell you something, however. I don't care what the police say, Rick didn't kill that man. I believe in him, as do many other people, and when this is all over and the cops find out the truth, Rick is going to know who his friends are and who stood by him when he was in trouble. I guess that won't be you."

Roberta sniffed. "I'm surprised at you, Clara. I thought you had more intelligence and common sense than that. I feel sorry for you." She opened the door and marched outside.

Clara had a childish urge to stick out her tongue. Instead she stomped down the aisle to the Nook and poured herself a cup of coffee. In spite of what she'd said to Roberta, she had the uncomfortable feeling that most of the people in town would feel as Roberta did.

Some of them had already condemned Rick, and this would only reinforce their convictions. Many more would follow in their footsteps, if she didn't do something to prove that Mayor Carson Dexter was the one the police should have in custody.

She arrived home that evening to find Tatters once

more locked up in the utility room. He showed his appreciation for being freed by leaping up at her in an attempt to lick her face. His enthusiasm quite literally bowled her over, and she landed on her back in the hallway.

It reminded her of when Roberta landed in a heap on the street, and being reminded of Roberta did not put her in the best of moods. She yelled at the dog, who slunk away with his tail between his legs. Instantly regretting taking out her annoyance on Tatters, she went after him and found him curled up on her bed. It took a few minutes of soothing words and constant petting before he finally lifted his head and licked her face.

"I'm sorry, boy," she said, cuddling an arm around his neck. "You were so happy to see me, and I didn't mean to be such a grouch. How about we share a sandwich to make up for it?"

Tatters' ears pricked up, and he leapt from the bed, tail swishing back and forth. He followed her across the living room and into the kitchen, and stood close to her while she spread mayonnaise on bread and stuffed ham and cheese between the slices.

After opening a jar of pickles, she fished out a couple and added them to the plate. "That's good enough," she muttered, and Tatters whined in response.

She had just finished eating and was cleaning up the kitchen when the doorbell rang, making Tatters bark. He rushed over to the front door and stood there, waiting expectantly with quivering ears as Clara opened the door.

Stephanie stepped forward and then halted as Tatters

uttered a low growl. "Wow," she murmured. "Good watchdog."

"It's all right, boy." Clara smoothed the ruffled hair on the back of the dog's neck. "She's family."

Tatters stopped growling and started wagging his tail instead.

"Impressive." Stephanie stepped into the hallway and closed the door. "He understood what you said."

Clara smiled. "Tatters, this is my cousin, Stephanie. Steffie, meet Tatters."

Tatters sat down and offered his paw.

Stephanie gaped, and even Clara felt a jolt of surprise. "You'd better shake it," she said, "or you'll offend him."

Stephanie gingerly grasped the paw and gave it a little shake. "Pleased to meet you."

Tatters yawned, got up and strolled back into the living room.

"He gets bored easily," Clara said, watching her cousin's eyebrows rise.

"I guess so." Grinning, Stephanie followed the dog into the living room.

"You want a cup of coffee?" Clara crossed the room to the kitchen.

"What, no wine?"

"I was hoping you'd say that." She opened the fridge and took out a bottle. "I just happen to have a bottle of chardonnay on hand."

"Good." Stephanie walked over to the table and sat down. "So, how are you holding up?"

"Not bad, all things considered." Clara pulled out the cork with a loud *pop* that made Tatters jump.

Stephanie watched him in amusement. "You were right. He's a big dog."

"Tell me about it. You want to try sleeping with him."

"No, thanks. I have enough trouble fighting George for the covers." Stephanie held out her hand to the dog and received a wet lick. "How does Aunt Jessie get along with him?"

"She adores him, though she'd be the last one to admit it." Clara brought two wineglasses to the table and sat down. "She keeps threatening to ban him from the house, but I know she'd be devastated if anything happened to him. I think she enjoys the company. She's been lonely since Dad died."

"Oh, I thought she was going out with Tony Manetas."

Clara rolled her eyes. "Bite your tongue. I wouldn't want that man for a stepfather."

Stephanie laughed. "He's harmless. Just obvious, that's all. Besides, I can't see Aunt Jessie allowing anyone to get the better of her." She took a sip of wine and nodded her appreciation. "Do you think she'll ever get married again?"

Clara felt a stab of apprehension. "I don't know. I don't want her to be lonely, but I'd hate to see her tied to someone who might make her unhappy."

"What about you? Don't you want to get married?"

Clara frowned. "When did this get to be about me? What kind of question is that?"

Stephanie gazed at her over the rim of her glass. "You're not getting any younger, you know."

"Thanks. I'm only thirty-one. Not exactly ancient."

"Like I said before, I just don't want you to let one bad experience put you off ever getting married."

"I'll bear that in mind."

Obviously realizing that she was pushing the wrong buttons, Stephanie put down her glass. "All right, tell me why you wanted me to come over tonight."

Thankful for the change in subject, Clara told her everything she'd learned from her research on the computer.

When she was done, she sat back, anxiously waiting for her cousin's reaction.

"Wow," Stephanie said, her eyes wide with shock. "It does look like Carson Dexter could be the killer." She paused, apparently thinking it over. "But the *mayor*, Clara. How are we ever going to convince Dan of that?"

"I was hoping you'd come up with one of your brilliant ideas."

"You always say my ideas get us into trouble."

"Well, now and then you come up with a good one. I—" She broke off as Tatters uttered a menacing growl. "What is it, boy?"

Tatters got up, ears quivering and tail standing straight up like a banner.

"Yoo-hoo! I'm home!"

Clara rolled her eyes as Jessie's voice rang out from the hallway.

Tatters barked in excitement and tore out of the kitchen.

Stephanie looked amused. "Do you think he'll flatten her?"

"He might. He did me when I got home tonight."

"You're kidding." Stephanie turned her head. "Sounds like Aunt Jessie has things under control."

From the hallway came the sound of scuffling and Jessie's laughter.

"She always has things under control," Clara muttered. She got up from the table. "Guess we'll have to finish this conversation later."

Stephanie got up, too. "Don't worry, Clara. We'll think of something." She couldn't say any more as Jessie poked her head in the kitchen doorway. "Oh, there you are. Hello, Stephanie, dear. I thought I recognized your car." She looked around. "George and the kids didn't come with you?"

"No, I just popped in to . . . ah . . . discuss business at the store." Stephanie walked over to her aunt and gave her a hug. "How are you?"

"Wonderful. How are the children? I haven't seen them in ages."

"I'll have you over for dinner real soon." Stephanie turned to Clara. "It's your day off tomorrow. Make the most of it."

Interpreting the hidden message, Clara nodded. "I'll try."

"You don't have to leave yet, do you?" Jessie walked

with Stephanie to the hallway. "Can't you stay and chat for a while?"

"I wish I could." Stephanie glanced at her watch. "I should get back. The kids always take advantage of George when I'm not there, and heaven knows what they are up to by now."

"George is a grown man. He should be able to take care of his own kids."

Stephanie smiled. "You'd think. The truth is, he's a pushover with them and they know it."

Jessie shook her head. "I still find it hard to believe that you're the mother of three children. It doesn't seem all that long ago that you two were kids yourselves." She closed her eyes and clutched her heart. "I hope to goodness your children are easier to handle than you two were. You were never happy unless you were playing tricks on someone or other."

Stephanie laughed. "I guess we were a bit unruly."

"Unruly?" Jessie shook her head. "My dear, you two were holy terrors. I still shudder every time I remember the night you convinced your babysitter she was seeing a ghost and just about gave her a heart attack. She never came near this house again. What's more, she told all her friends. Your mother and I had the devil of a time trying to find a babysitter after that."

"She was an idiot. Any sane person could tell it wasn't a ghost." Stephanie opened the front door. "Thanks for the wine, Clara."

Jessie twisted her head around to look at Clara. "Wine? Any left?"

"Half a bottle." Clara nodded in the direction of the kitchen. "Help yourself."

Waving good-night to Stephanie, Jessie disappeared into the living room.

"Don't worry," Stephanie whispered. "We'll work something out. Just enjoy your day off tomorrow."

"I'll try," Clara promised, though she could see the day stretching ahead of her with nothing to do but worry about Rick.

She closed the door and went hunting for Tatters' leash. A walk along the beach would help clear her mind and perhaps give her some ideas of what to do next. Right then she couldn't seem to think about anything except Rick on a narrow cot in a holding cell, scared out of his mind.

Had he been formally charged? she wondered. The sound of the TV tempted her to watch the news with her mother, but she dismissed the idea. The last thing she needed tonight was another long discussion on how stupid she was to believe a man innocent, despite all the evidence pointing otherwise.

Poking her head around the living room door, she announced, "I'm taking the dog for a walk. I won't be long."

Jessie nodded and waved her wineglass at her. "I'll just finish this and then I'm going to bed. Oh, by the way, I suppose you heard that your hardware man has been arrested."

"Yes, I did. Good-night, Mother." Clara withdrew her head, called out to Tatters and was out the door before she had time to hear her mother's answer.

The walk did little to chase away her troubled thoughts, and she spent a restless night tossing around in her bed. She awoke the next morning to the sound of Tatters barking and the doorbell ringing frantically. It took her a moment or two to remember it was her day off, and she considered ignoring the doorbell. The persistent pealing was annoying, however, and with a muttered curse she fell out of bed and dragged on her robe.

Outside in the hallway, Tatters leapt up and down, his deep barks sending shafts of pain through her head. She gave him a sharp command as she headed for the front door and pulled it open.

Stephanie stood on the front step, her face glowing with excitement. "I've got the greatest idea! I really think it will work if we—" She broke off, her gaze traveling down Clara's body as if just noticing her for the first time. "Oh crap. Did I wake you up?"

"You probably woke up the entire neighborhood." Clara peered down the street, to where a teenager dragged a buzzing lawn mower across a front lawn. "What's the time, anyway?"

Stephanie glanced at her watch. "It's a little after nine. Sorry. I keep forgetting you sleep late."

"It's okay. Come in. I'll get us some coffee." Clara closed the door behind her cousin. "Maybe then I can get my brain to function." She led the way into the living room, then paused when a thought struck her. "Why aren't you at the store? There isn't any more news, is there? About Rick, I mean."

"No, not that I've heard, anyway." Stephanie followed her into the kitchen and sat down at the table. "That's not why I'm here. I thought it better to talk about this in person than on the phone."

"Talk about what?"

"You asked me to come up with an idea of how we can prove the mayor killed Frank Tomeski."

Jessie had left the coffeepot on, and Clara emptied it into two mugs. Carrying them over to the table, she asked, "So what's the idea?"

Stephanie looked a little sheepish. "Well, it's kind of complicated. Maybe you should drink your coffee first."

Frowning, Clara opened the fridge and took out a carton of milk. Stephanie's ideas were notorious for being impractical at best and downright dangerous at worst. Already Clara was having qualms about it. She handed Stephanie the milk and sat down. The coffee tasted bitter and wasn't all that hot, but it woke her up enough to listen to her cousin's latest brain wave.

Stephanie took her time pouring milk into her coffee. She sipped it and pulled a face before putting the mug down. "I love Aunt Jessie dearly, but she makes the worst coffee I ever tasted."

"How do you know she made it?"

"Because you just fell out of bed."

"Oh, right." Clara ran a hand through her tangled hair. "I must look a mess."

Stephanie grinned. "I wouldn't suggest paying Rick Sanders a visit looking like that."

Clara decided to ignore the insult and said instead, "Which brings us to your idea. So, tell me."

Stephanie drew in a long breath. "All right. Remember what Aunt Jessie said last night about us making our babysitter think she was seeing a ghost?"

"Yeah, I think I can remember that far back."

Stephanie sighed. "Well, I thought we could make Carson Dexter think he was seeing the ghost of Amy Tomeski coming to haunt him. It might unnerve him enough for him to confess what he did."

Clara stared at her. "Are you *nuts*? Our babysitter was a gullible teenager. Carson Dexter is a grown man and, if we're right, a dangerous killer. How on earth are we going to fool him?"

Stephanie pouted. "I don't think the mayor is a dangerous killer. I think he might have gotten caught up in the circumstances and did something he wouldn't normally do. I think he's probably scared right now, and if we can catch him off guard, we might get him to say something that would give us the proof we need."

Clara stared at her over the rim of her coffee mug. "You know, sometimes you actually make sense."

"Thank you."

"But I still don't see how in the world we're going to convince him he's seeing Amy Tomeski's ghost."

Stephanie leaned forward, her eyes gleaming. "That's the interesting part. I looked up that article you mentioned on the Internet. Did you see the pic of Amy?"

"Yes, I did. She looks nothing like her brother." Clara frowned. "Of course, her brother was dead when they took his picture, so—"

"Clara." Stephanie pulled her hair back with both hands. "Did she remind you of anyone?"

"No." Clara looked harder at her cousin. "Why?"

"She was short, blonde and"—Stephanie looked down at her stomach—"just a little overweight."

Clara put down her mug. "Wait a minute."

"No, listen." Stephanie held up her hand. "We can find those huge black earrings like the ones she was wearing in the photo, in one of the souvenir shops. I'll tie my hair up like this." She bunched up her hair again and pulled it back. "Huh? What do you think?"

Clara studied her, doubts crowding her mind. "Well, maybe you do look a little like her but—"

"You know that black and white striped tank top she was wearing? Well, George has a golf shirt with the same kind of stripes. I can cut out the sleeves and collar, and wear jeans like she did, and I'll look enough like her to fool Carson Dexter. After all, he hasn't seen her in what . . . five years? Six?"

Clara's pulse started racing, the way it did when she knew she was about to do something really stupid. "I suppose . . . if we're in a dark place somewhere, but—"

"This is what we do."

Stephanie was in full throttle now, and knowing there was no stopping her, Clara lapsed into silence.

"We call Carson Dexter from a pay phone and tell him that someone from his past wants to meet him at midnight in the community hall. George has a key to the hall, for when he coaches basketball there. We'll turn off the main lights from the fuse box and just leave the stage lamps on. They're on a different circuit."

"How do you know all that?"

Stephanie made a face. "I've spent enough time messing around with that stuff while George was busy with the kids.

"What if he doesn't come?"

"We make it sound like he'll be in deep trouble if he doesn't."

"What if he brings Dan with him?"

"And risk being arrested for murder? I don't think so."

Clara struggled with her conscience for a moment longer. "It sounds all right on the surface, but—"

"If we stop and worry about what could go wrong, we'll never get anywhere." Stephanie picked up her mug again. "Don't you want to clear Rick's name?"

"Well, of course I do. But what if we're wrong about Carson Dexter? What if he's not the killer after all?"

"I guess we'll find out tonight."

Clara swallowed too fast and choked. "Tonight?"

"We have to strike fast. Besides, today is your day off. It will give us time to get done what we need to do."

"What about the store?"

"Molly can take care of it. We're always slow at the beginning of the week." Stephanie glanced at the clock. "I'd better get back and cut up George's shirt. You see if you can find earrings that match the ones in the picture of Amy." She got up and headed for the living room. "We'll meet back here tonight. What time do you think we should call the mayor?"

"I don't know." Clara was getting more worried about the whole thing by the minute. "We have to give him enough time to get down to the community hall, and give us enough time to get there before him."

"Okay, I'll meet you back here at ten."

Clara followed her across the room while Tatters hovered hopefully by the front door. "What about George?"

"What about him?" Stephanie paused in the act of opening the door. "I'm not going to tell him what we're planning, if that's what you think."

"No, of course not. How are you going to explain, though, about going out at ten o'clock at night? Where will you tell him you're going?"

Stephanie frowned. "I'll think of something. You'd better think of something to tell Aunt Jessie."

Clara shook her head. "I don't know, Steffie. This all seems a bit risky. We could end up in a lot of trouble."

Stephanie grinned. "Reminds you of the old days, doesn't it?"

"Too much. Still, if it helps put Carson Dexter in jail instead of Rick, I guess it's worth the risk."

"That's my cousin!" Stephanie gave her a sharp nudge

with her elbow. "I was beginning to think that New York had taken away all your spirit."

"More like it taught me to use common sense." Clara sighed. "Something tells me we're going to regret this, but for what it's worth, I'm in. With both feet."

"Great." Stephanie leapt down the steps. "See you tonight!"

Clara closed the door and leaned on it. What had she done? Got carried away by one of Stephanie's wild schemes again, that's what.

Tatters sat at her feet, looked up at her and whined.

"Good idea," she muttered. "But first I have to shower, dress and eat." She headed for the bathroom, trying not to think about all the things that could go wrong with their plan. *Best not think about it at all,* she told herself, as she turned on the faucet in the shower. Otherwise she'd be a basket case by the time her cousin got there that night. Judging from experience, this adventure could well end up in total disaster.

14

An hour or so later Clara fastened the leash to Tatters' collar and the two of them took off down the street. This time she walked along the boardwalk, where tourists hovered in front of noisy arcades, souvenir shops and fast-food stands.

The aroma of pizza, hot dogs and lobster rolls mingled with the salty smell of seaweed and sand, and screeching children dodged in and out of the crowd. Tatters seemed unmoved by all the activity, content to sniff the air as he trotted ahead of his owner.

Pausing beneath a blue and white striped awning, Clara peered in the window of a quaint gift shop. An assortment of seashells and ships in bottles shared room with miniature lighthouses and delicate sculptures of seagulls and whales.

"This looks promising," Clara murmured. She tied Tatters' leash to a railing in front of the window and told him to stay. "You'll get a cookie if you don't move or make a sound," she told him. Tatters looked worried but obediently sat, his ears flat against his head—a sure sign he wasn't too happy.

"I won't be long." Clara gave him a final pat and hurried into the store. Walking rapidly along the shelves, she passed small stands of fridge ornaments and calendars with pictures of the shoreline. She knew she was getting warmer when she spotted a display of ornamental combs and barrettes. At the next counter she hit pay dirt: trays loaded with earrings of all shapes and sizes.

Large black ones had to be in fashion, as she found an assortment of them. None of them matched the ones Amy Tomeski was wearing in her photo, but Clara found ones that were close to the shape and size. She had just swiped her credit card when she heard an uproar outside. Someone was shouting amid the frantic barking of a dog.

"I'll be right back," she told the startled assistant, and rushed out of the store.

A little crowd had gathered outside, and Clara had to push her way through to see the source of all the commotion. Her stomach dropped when she saw Tatters, hair raised on his neck and barking furiously at the young man he had cornered against the window.

"Tatters! How could you! *Bad* boy!" She darted forward and grabbed the dog's collar.

Tatters stopped barking and emitted low growls instead. His ears quivered with indignation and a long ridge of hair stood upright on his back.

"I'm so sorry," Clara said as the scared-looking teen edged around them. "I don't know why he's behaving like this. I hope he didn't hurt you."

The young man didn't answer. He just dipped his head, shoved his way through the crowd and disappeared.

"He tried to steal your dog," a woman said as the rest of the people gradually wandered off. "He untied the leash, and the minute he tried to pull the dog away, it started barking and snapping at him." She looked down at Tatters and smiled. "That's a smart dog. He knew he didn't want to go with that nasty man."

Clara's mouth felt dry as she realized how close she'd come to losing Tatters. "Thank you," she told the woman. "I wonder if you'd do me a big favor? I have to go back into the store to get something. I hate to ask, but I don't want to leave Tatters alone again—"

"Of course I'll hold him." The woman smiled and held out her hand for the leash. "I love dogs. We'll get along just fine."

"That's so kind of you. I'll be as quick as I can." Clara handed over the leash and dashed back into the store. The assistant had the earrings in a bag all ready to go, and handed her the receipt. Clara smiled her thanks and ran out of the store again, half-afraid she'd find the woman had left and taken Tatters with her.

Her relief made her limp when she saw the dog where she'd left him, happily watching a group of children chase a kite down the beach.

With a smile, the woman handed the leash back to her. "You work in the Raven's Nest, don't you?" she said when Clara thanked her. "I remember seeing you in there the other day. I stopped in to buy my niece that latest vampire book that's all the rage."

Clara smiled. "Yes, I work there. My cousin owns the store."

"Oh, you're Stephanie's cousin?" The woman shook her head. "I'm afraid I'm not a big reader. I don't have much time to read, so I don't go into the store that much." She paused, then added, "You must know Rick Sanders, then? He owns Parson's Hardware across the street."

Clara felt her spine going rigid. Making an effort to keep the tension out of her voice, she said, "I know him well."

"Such a shame." The woman looked around, then leaned forward. "If you ask me, someone is framing him for that murder. Rick Sanders isn't a killer. I just know it."

Clara relaxed. "Thank you," she said, feeling like hugging the woman. "I'm so happy to meet someone who feels the same way."

"Oh, I do." The woman shook her head. "I'm quite sure a lot of others think so, too. Carson Dexter should be ashamed of himself. He's the one who kept insisting

Dan Petersen arrest Rick. I don't think Rick would be in jail now if it weren't for the mayor's accusations."

"Well, let's hope the truth comes out eventually." Clara gave Tatters a tug. "It was very nice talking to you."

"You, too." The woman smiled and patted Tatters' head. "You take care of your mistress, that's a good dog." She looked up. "You never have to worry about anything as long as that dog is with you. He'll take good care of you, I can tell." With a wave she was gone, leaving Clara staring after her.

Smart woman.

Jolted once more by the dog's thoughts echoing in her head, Clara shook her head at him.

Of course. She should have thought of it herself. She'd take Tatters along with her to the community hall that night. Carson Dexter would have a tough time doing them harm with the dog there to protect them.

Feeling a little better, she headed for the beach. Tatters deserved a good run after everything he'd been through that morning. Leaping ahead of her, Tatters apparently agreed.

Shortly before ten that evening, Clara announced to her mother that she was taking the dog for a long walk. Jessie answered with a sleepy, "Have fun. I'm going to bed."

Clara led Tatters out to the street, hoping fervently that her mother would fall asleep immediately and wouldn't notice that her daughter hadn't arrived home by midnight.

The last thing she needed was a hysterical Jessie calling the cops to say her daughter was missing.

Hoping that she'd find Stephanie waiting for her, Clara set off for the library.

———

Stephanie glanced at the clock on her bedside table and winced. She was supposed to meet Clara in ten minutes and she still didn't have George's key to the community hall. She stuffed her husband's mutilated golf shirt into the backpack on her bed and tugged on the zipper. Excitement made her fingers shake and she had trouble getting it closed.

Just then George's voice called out from the hallway. "Steff? Are you in the bathroom?"

Crap. Stephanie shoved the bag under the bed. "I'm in here. What's wrong?"

George appeared in the doorway. "Michael can't find his Darth Vader mask."

"Tell him to look under his bed. That's where he hides most of his stuff." She gave the backpack a guilty push with the toe of her shoe. Staring at the bedside clock, she added, "I have to go and pick up Clara. She's going to help me tonight."

George frowned. "I sometimes wonder if that bookstore is worth all the trouble. I hate to think of you working half the night and then having to get up early to go back there the next morning."

"It's okay, hon. I don't have to do it that often."

"It doesn't seem that long ago since you took the last inventory."

Stephanie walked over to him, grabbed the collar of his shirt and dragged his face down to meet hers. "You worry too much. I'll be just fine." She kissed him on the mouth and let him go. "Be a sweetheart and go see if you can find Darth Vader's mask for Michael. Please?"

He grinned. "When you kiss me like that I'd rob a bank for you."

She pretended to be shocked. "George Henry Dowd! You could never do anything that criminal."

"You'd be surprised what I could do." He leered at her and sauntered out the door.

Shaking her head, Stephanie reached for the backpack. George would be surprised himself if he knew what she was about to do. She felt another guilty pang. It was so wrong to lie to her husband. Then again, it was for a good cause.

Having reassured herself, she shoved the strap of the backpack over her shoulder and stole out into the hallway. She could hear George in Michael's bedroom, arguing with his son. Deciding it would be safer to go out the back way, she sped into the kitchen, swiped George's keys from their hook on the wall and tore out the door.

It took only a moment to throw the backpack into the back seat of her car. She softly closed the door, then hurried back to the kitchen. Leaning against the wall for a moment, she let out her breath. All she had to do now was kiss her husband and children, and go trap a killer.

———

Three blocks down from her house Clara spotted Stephanie's car waiting at the curb outside the library. Her cousin had a look of horror on her face when she opened the door. "What are you doing? You can't bring that dog in here! I've got allergies."

"Since when?" Clara opened the back door and urged Tatters to jump onto the backseat. He ecstatically obliged, and settled himself down with a smug look on his face.

"All right, I don't, but my kids do. They'll be sneezing all over the place tomorrow."

"They won't if you vacuum out the car when you get home."

"Oh, yes, that's a very good idea. I can just imagine George when he sees me vacuuming the car late at night after I'm supposed to have been at the store taking inventory."

Clara raised her eyebrows. "You told him that one again?"

Stephanie's jaw jutted in the light from the streetlamp. "Yes, I did. He doesn't keep count of how many times I take inventory."

"Just as well." Clara climbed into the front seat. "You'd never get away with it if he did."

"It's not like I make a habit of it. I—" Stephanie broke

off and glared at her cousin. "Don't change the subject. Why on earth did you bring that monster with you?"

"He's not a monster." Clara dug in her pocket and pulled out a dog treat. Twisting around, she held it out, and Tatters snapped it up, licked his lips and waited for more. "I brought him along for security. He's our bodyguard."

Stephanie snorted. "That dog? He's more likely to bowl over the mayor and lick his face."

"Meanwhile, we make our escape."

"Oh." Stephanie considered it. "I guess that might work."

"He might surprise you." Clara stretched out a hand to pat the dog's head. "He fought off a would-be kidnapper this morning."

Stephanie gasped. "Someone tried to kidnap you?"

"Not me. Tatters. I left him outside the store while I went in to buy those ridiculous earrings." Clara relayed the story of Tatters' near abduction while her cousin steered the car down the hill toward the harbor.

When she was finished, Stephanie uttered a low laugh. "Good old Tatters. He wasn't going to let anyone get the better of him. I guess that makes him officially a member of the Quinn family."

"He does fit in rather well." Clara glanced over her shoulder. Tatters sat staring out of the window, no doubt wondering when he was going to finish his walk.

"What did you tell Aunt Jessie about tonight?"

Stephanie pulled up in the harbor parking lot and cut off the engine.

"I told her I was taking the dog for a walk." Clara paused. "I just hope she doesn't wake up and wonder what's taking me so long."

Stephanie patted her arm. "Don't worry. She'll be fast asleep by now and won't even know you're gone."

"I don't know. I keep worrying that she'll wake up and realize I'm not home. She could call Dan. That would mess up everything."

"She won't wake up. You're always telling me how she sleeps like a drunken sailor. Even if she does, she won't get out of bed. Even if she does get out of bed, she won't go to your room, so how's she going to know you're not there?"

"I don't know. I just have a real uneasy feeling about all this."

"Of course you do. We're trying to trap a murderer into confessing to his crime. That's not exactly something we do every day. I'm nervous, too." Stephanie opened her door. "We have to make this call soon if we want Carson to be at the community hall by midnight."

"What are you going to say to him?"

Stephanie paused in the act of climbing out of the car. "Me? I'm the ideas person, remember? You're the one who does all the talking."

"You know I'm not good at this." Clara ran her fingers through her bangs. "How am I going to convince him to meet us?"

Stephanie sighed. "You just tell him that someone from his past has something important to tell him and wants to meet him at midnight. Tell him that if he wants to avoid a whole lot of trouble, he'd better be there and to come alone." Stephanie finished climbing out, then leaned down to peer at her. "Make it sound real mysterious and threatening."

"Mysterious and threatening. Wonderful." Clara cracked open the window and got out. Tatters stood up, wagging his tail. "Not you, boy. You've got to stay. We won't be long." She closed the door and waited for her cousin to join her.

"There's a pay phone over there." Stephanie pointed across the parking lot to the gas station, where two phone booths stood side by side at the corner of the convenience store. "Did you bring change for the phone?"

Clara pulled a handful of coins from her pocket.

"Good thing." Stephanie set off for the phone booth. "I'd forgotten we'd need change until just now. I haven't used a pay phone since we were in our teens."

She darted across the street, and Clara followed, trying frantically to think of what she would say to the mayor.

Stephanie opened the door of the phone booth. "It smells like crap in here."

Clara stepped inside, wrinkling her nose at the putrid smell of stale tobacco and something she didn't want to think about. She picked up the receiver and held it an inch from her ear. "There's no dial tone."

Stephanie looked stunned. "You're kidding. What do we do now?"

"We try the one next door." Clara slammed the phone back on its rest. Following her cousin to the other phone booth, she wondered if perhaps it was a sign that they should forget the whole thing and go home.

Inside the booth, she lifted the receiver, listened for a moment, then nodded. "This one's okay." She felt in her pocket for the slip of paper on which she'd scribbled the mayor's phone number. Handing it to Stephanie, she added, "Read this out for me."

Stephanie held it up to catch the light from the store next door. "Where did you get this?"

"From the City Hall website. It's a direct number he put up there so that citizens could call him to discuss issues. Part of his Senate campaign, I guess."

"Good going!"

There wasn't a lot of room for both of them in the narrow phone booth, and Clara had to keep her elbows pressed to her sides as she dropped coins into the slot. The phone clicked, and the dial tone returned. As her cousin read out the numbers, Clara punched them out on the keypad, then waited, heart pounding, for Carson Dexter to answer.

When the deep voice said "Hello?" in her ear, she jumped violently, nearly dropping the phone. Eyes wide, she stared at Stephanie, momentarily brain-dead.

Her cousin flapped an impatient hand at her, and Clara made a supreme effort to gather her thoughts.

"Hello?" the mayor said again, and this time he sounded annoyed.

Clara swallowed, then lowered her voice to a husky growl. "Am I speaking to Mayor Dexter?"

"Yes, you are. It's a little late to be calling me. What do you want?"

Clara lowered her voice even more. "I have a message for you. Someone from your past wishes to meet you. Be at the community hall at midnight tonight."

There was a long pause, then the mayor asked abruptly, "Who *is* this?"

"Never mind who I am." Clara signaled at Stephanie with her raised eyebrows and received another flap of the hand in response. "I . . . suggest you be there if you want to avoid some real trouble."

"I'm not going anywhere unless you tell me who you are and what you want."

He'd sounded as if he were on the verge of hanging up. Panicking, Clara once more signaled at Stephanie.

This time even her cousin looked uncertain.

Clara tried again. "The person who wants to meet you has information about the death of Frank Tomeski. If you're not at the community hall by midnight, this person will take the information to the police. I don't think you want that to happen." She dropped the phone back on its rest and let out a shuddering breath.

"What did he say?" Stephanie's anxious eyes raked her cousin's face.

"I don't know." Realizing she was still speaking in the grating tone she'd used on the phone, she raised her voice.

"Er . . . I didn't hear what he said. I hung up before he could reply."

"Crap." Stephanie opened the door and stumbled out of the booth. "Now we don't know if he'll be there or not."

"Well, I can't call him back and ask him." Clara stepped out into the fresh night air and pulled in deep breaths. "We'll just have to go down there and hope he comes."

"All right. Let's get going. I have to get changed and everything."

Clara looked at her watch. "It's only ten thirty. We have plenty of time."

"Not if Carson Dexter decides to get there early." Stephanie set off across the street to the parking lot. "We need to be ready and waiting for him when he gets there."

Clara caught up with her as she reached the car. "Have you thought about what you're going to say as Amy?"

Stephanie opened the car door. "I was hoping you'd do all the talking."

"Me? You're the one playing the ghost."

"Yes, but you know more about Amy than I do. Besides, it will be even more creepy if the voice comes from somewhere else." She climbed in behind the wheel.

"So what the heck am I supposed to say?"

"I don't know. Something creepy."

Clara opened her mouth to argue, but Stephanie went on talking. "It's been five years since Carson last heard Amy's voice. He probably won't realize it's not hers."

Clara seriously doubted that, but things had gone too far now to back out. She slipped Tatters a dog treat and slid onto the passenger seat. "Come to think of it, how are we going to prove anything, even if Carson does say something to incriminate himself?"

Stephanie started the engine. "I thought about that. There's a security camera in the main hall. We'll have to make sure it's working."

"I could record what he says on my cell." Clara held it up so her cousin could see it. "It's got a pretty good camera on it."

"Great!" Stephanie glanced over her shoulder. "I just hope that dog is quiet. We don't want Carson to know that anyone else is there besides Amy."

"Tatters will be quiet. I'll have a word with him."

Stephanie threw her a resigned look. "Of course. I keep forgetting you talk to dogs. I just hope he does what he's told."

"Trust me. Tatters will be a great ally, you'll see."

"I hope you're right." Stephanie drove out of the parking lot and turned the car toward Main Street. "Because, if something goes wrong and we get caught, we could be in big trouble."

Clara felt an even deeper pang of apprehension. "Wait a minute. That's my line."

Stephanie shrugged. "We can't be certain of anything. We can only hope and pray it all goes as planned."

Clara leaned back on her seat. "*Now* she tells me."

"It'll be okay." Stephanie sounded less than sure,

rattling Clara's nerves even more. "We just have to keep our heads, that's all."

She was silent as she drove to the community hall, and Clara could only guess what she was thinking. She tried not to do much thinking herself. The scenarios she came up with were far too disturbing.

Stephanie parked the car two blocks from the community hall, down a side street sheltered by leafy oak trees. "You'll have to get the dog out of the car," she told Clara as she cut the engine. "I need to get into the backseat to change."

Clara climbed out and opened the back door. With an excited *Woof!* Tatters leapt from the car and started trotting down the street. Clara dashed after him, hissing at him to stop. He was halfway down the block before he obeyed.

Grabbing his collar, she led him back to the car. Stephanie was in the backseat, struggling into a widely striped tank top with a ragged neckline and armholes. "I didn't have time to hem it," she explained when Clara tilted her head to one side and gave her a quizzical look. "It looks all right, doesn't it?"

"Well, I wouldn't wear it to a wedding, but it'll pass in the dark."

She watched her cousin drag her hair back into two bunches and snap a rubber band on each. Digging into her enormous tapestry purse, Stephanie came up with a dark-colored lipstick and swiped it twice across her mouth.

In the cold light of the streetlamp her face looked as if it had been slashed with a meat cleaver.

Clara blinked. "What are you doing? You look like a massacred clown."

"That's the whole idea." Stephanie craned her neck to see herself in the rearview mirror. "I want to look scary."

"Well, it's working." Clara pulled a small envelope from her pocket and handed it to her cousin. "Here, you'll need these."

Stephanie opened the envelope and held up one of the huge black earrings. "Good job. These are perfect." She fastened them to her ears. "Now stand back a bit and look at me through the window." She pressed her face to the window and opened her eyes wide.

Clara backed up a few steps and studied her. "Did you bring mascara with you?"

"I did." Stephanie dug in her purse again. "I was hoping I wouldn't have to wear it. It's going to be hard to get it off before I get home. George will wonder what on earth I'm doing with all this makeup on."

"Stephanie, one way or another, he'll have to know what we did. If Carson Dexter confesses to murder, everyone is going to know how and where he was caught. If he doesn't confess, or isn't the killer after all, you and I will be in so much trouble the whole town will know about it."

Stephanie craned her neck again and leaned over the front seat. Dabbing on mascara, she murmured, "I guess you're right. There's no way we're going to get out of this without George knowing about it. I just hope he forgives me."

"He's forgiven you for every stupid thing you've ever done so far." Clara felt Tatters tug on his leash, and looked down at him. "Not now, boy. Later."

Tatters whined, and Clara squatted down so she could look him in the face. Taking his head between her hands, she said softly, "I need you to be a good boy, Tatters. You will have to be extra quiet and not make a sound until I say you can. Can you do that for me?"

Tatters licked her nose, and Clara stood up.

Stephanie dabbed a heavy blob of eye shadow all around her eyes, then found an eyeliner and ringed her eyes in black. Looking back at Clara, she asked, "How about now?"

Clara backed up again and caught her breath. In the shadowy light Stephanie looked just like the picture of Amy Tomeski. "Perfect." She moved back to the car. "Absolutely perfect."

Stephanie grinned. "I knew it. Now let's get into that hall before Carson Dexter gets there. Did you remember to bring a flashlight?"

Clara held up her key ring. Dangling from it was a mini LED flashlight.

Stephanie nodded her approval, then locked the car before starting down the street at a brisk pace.

Clara followed with Tatters trotting along at her side, sniffing the air now and then.

The main door to the community hall was on a side street, and no one passed them as Stephanie used George's key to open the door and they slipped inside.

Switching on her flashlight, Clara directed the tiny beam down the hallway. "What's to stop Carson Dexter from switching on the lights?" she muttered as they made their way to the main hall.

"I know where to find the fuse box, remember? We'll switch off the circuit breakers."

Impressed, Clara followed her cousin to a small closet at the end of the hallway. Stephanie opened the door and focused her flashlight on a large fuse box fastened to the closet wall. She yanked the box's metal cover aside and trained the beam of light on the contents, peering at the rows until she found what she wanted. Flipping three of the switches, she murmured, "This should take care of the lights. All that will go on now are the footlights on the stage and the security camera."

Clara followed her through the doors that led to the main hall, where Stephanie flipped a switch by the side of the stage. A row of lamps glowed along the lower edge of the stage floor.

Clara glanced around the big hall for a suitable hiding place. "Looks like the best place to hide is up on the stage behind the curtains."

"I guess so." Stephanie held back, her face a mask of worry.

Clara peered at her. "You're not going to chicken out now, are you?"

"No, of course not. It's just . . ." Her voice trailed off and she put a hand over her mouth.

Alarmed, Clara moved closer. "It's just what? What are you not telling me?"

"Nothing." Stephanie shook her head. "It's just that if we're wrong and the mayor isn't the killer, this could really mess things up. I mean, he's the *mayor*, for heaven's sake. George could lose his job." Her voice rose on a wail. "I could lose the store!"

Clara gritted her teeth. "It's a bit late to think about that now. Do you want to forget this and go home? You'd better tell me now."

Stephanie stared at her for a long moment, eyes wide and scared. Then she shook her head. "No. We've come this far. Let's get on with it." She twisted around and headed for the steps.

Heaving a sigh of relief, Clara followed, dragging a reluctant Tatters up the steps. The curtains smelled musty as she joined Stephanie behind them. "I hope Carson gets here soon," she muttered. "There's enough dust in these things to fill a tanker. We'll both be sneezing our heads off before long."

Stephanie didn't answer her. She was staring out across the stage to the darkened hall beyond.

Anxious that her cousin might still be panicking, Clara whispered, "What's wrong?"

"There's just one problem." Stephanie pointed into the darkness. "With the footlights on, we can't see into the hall. We won't know when the mayor gets here."

"We'll just have to rely on our ears, then." Clara squinted into the shadows. "We should hear him come in if we're quiet. Or Tatters will."

"He won't bark, will he?"

"Of course not." Clara crossed her fingers.

"What's the time?" Stephanie gave her cousin a nudge. "Isn't your watch luminous?"

Clara studied her wrist. "Quarter past eleven."

"Crap. We have to wait another forty-five minutes."

"I'm hungry."

"Me, too. We should have brought food with us."

At the mention of food Tatters stirred by Clara's side, and she quickly patted his head. "Not yet, boy. I promise you'll get a treat when all this is over."

The next half hour or so crawled by while Clara, seated on the floor with her cousin, did her best to keep a whispered conversation going. Stephanie's voice kept trailing off as if she were on the point of falling asleep.

"Maybe we should stand up," Clara said when Stephanie failed to answer her question. "This isn't going to work if we're both asleep when Carson Dexter gets here."

Stephanie mumbled something, and Clara gave her a hard shake. "Wake up. Come on, stand up." She scrambled to her feet and hauled Stephanie up with her.

"It's all right for you," Stephanie mumbled. "You're used to staying up half the night. It's way past my bedtime. I—"

"Shhh!" Clara pressed her hand over Stephanie's mouth. "Listen."

From somewhere in the hall outside came the unmistakable sound of a door closing.

In the glow from the lamps, Clara could see her cousin's eyes widen as she gave her a nod. Then her expression changed.

"Crap!"

Clara swiftly put a hand over Stephanie's mouth. "Shhh."

Behind her fingers, Stephanie whispered, "We forgot to check the security camera."

Dropping her hand, Clara felt in her pocket for her cell phone. She flipped it open and held it up so her cousin could see it, then waited, one hand on the back of Tatters' neck.

Moments later she heard a faint squeak as one of the doors into the hall opened. She felt the hair rising on Tatters' neck and gave him a little warning shake. She could feel him quivering, but much to her relief, he remained silent.

She could see Stephanie's face. She looked ghastly, like something out of a horror movie. Even if she hadn't resembled the dead Amy Tomeski, the image would have been enough to scare the heck out of anyone. Her cousin's eyes were wide, and her bottom lip was caught between her teeth. Stephanie was obviously scared to death herself.

From across the room came a low curse.

It was showtime, and the star performer appeared to be frozen to the spot.

15

Clara gave her cousin a sharp nudge with her elbow.

Stephanie blinked but still didn't move.

"Is anybody there?"

The gruff voice of the mayor made them both jump.

Clara put her hand on Stephanie's arm and gave her a push.

"You've got ten seconds," the mayor said, "then I'm leaving."

"I'm here!" Clara cringed as her voice came out much too high-pitched.

Stephanie uttered a tiny whimper, and Clara flapped a hand at her.

"Who are you? What do you want?"

Clara made a face at her cousin, who still hadn't moved. "I want to know why you killed my brother." This time she gave Stephanie a hearty shove, sending her forward through the curtain.

There was a long pause, then the mayor's voice, sounding incredulous, spoke again. "Amy?"

Clara's heart skipped a beat. She pointed the cell phone through the gap in the curtains. Making her voice as quavering as possible, she moaned, "I'm here to avenge Frank's death."

"I thought you were dead." The mayor's voice sounded closer, filling Clara with alarm. She couldn't see Stephanie and could only hope her cousin was playing her part.

Panic rising, she forced herself to speak again. "You left me as soon as you heard I was having your baby. How could you do that? It's your fault I'm dead. I'm going to punish you, Carson Dexter. You are going to die a horrible death and I'll see you in hell." It all sounded so ridiculous, like a very bad melodrama. There was no way the mayor was going to swallow it.

Just at that moment, Stephanie apparently recovered from her stage fright. She let out a hollow moan that seemed to echo through the rafters. Whatever else she was doing must have totally unnerved Carson Dexter. He uttered a shrill yelp of fear.

"Go away! Leave me alone. It was Frank's fault. He tried to blackmail me! He was going to tell my wife about us."

"So you killed him."

On the other side of the curtain, Stephanie uttered another moan.

"I didn't mean to kill him! He wouldn't believe I didn't have the money to pay him. He came at me with a hammer. I got it away from him, and the next thing I knew I was hitting him with it. He went down like a sack of potatoes."

"You put his body in Rick Sanders's truck."

"Yes, I had to hide it somewhere . . . wait a minute."

The voice, stronger now, drew closer. Clara put her hand through the gap and tried to feel for Stephanie.

"Who the hell are you?"

He was right in front of the stage, and he sounded furious. Thoroughly panicked, Clara hauled the curtain aside and grabbed hold of Stephanie. "Let's get out of here!"

"Wait a minute. You're not going anywhere." With surprising agility, the mayor leapt for the steps and bounded up them.

Stephanie whimpered, but the sound was drowned out by a ferocious growl.

Clara had forgotten about Tatters. The dog made a beeline for the mayor, and before he could react, Tatters had him on the ground, one paw in the middle of his chest and his snarling jaws inches from his face.

Clara thumbed out 911 on her cell and held it to her ear. The night dispatcher answered her. Quickly she gave him a brief rundown of what had happened.

Meanwhile, Carson was pleading with Stephanie to call off the dog. "No way," she said, her voice still not quite steady. "Not until the cops get here."

"You'd better turn the lights back on," Clara said, slipping the phone back into her pocket.

"Good idea." Stephanie disappeared, leaving Clara alone with the mayor.

"Look, I'm sure we can come to some arrangement," Carson said. He raised his head to look at her, and Tatters growled again, making him smack his head back down on the stage floor. "Just call the dog off. I'll give you whatever you want."

"You don't have anything I want," Clara muttered. "No, wait. What I want is to see you in jail instead of the man you tried to frame for murder."

"I didn't try to frame anyone. I just happened to see the truck there and figured it was a good place to hide the body. I didn't know who owned it." He peered up at her. "Who the hell are you, anyway?"

Clara smiled. "A good friend of Rick Sanders."

Just then, light flooded the hall, making her blink. Stephanie appeared in the doorway as the wail of a siren broke the silence outside.

"The cops are here," Stephanie said, waving a hand at the hallway behind her. She walked across the hall, and a moment later, Dan burst through the doorway with Tim, his deputy, hot on his heels.

Tim rushed over to the stage and up the steps, pausing as Tatters uttered a warning growl.

"It's all right, boy," Clara said softly, "you can let him up now."

The dog lifted his paw and stepped away from the mayor.

Dan slowly made his way up the steps to the stage, disbelief on his face.

Carson sat up, running a hand through his hair. "Dan! Thank God you got here. These idiots and their dog attacked me for no reason whatsoever. I'm charging them with assault. I insist you arrest them right now."

Dan seemed uncomfortable as he looked at Clara, then Stephanie, then back to Carson. "What's going on here, Carson?"

"He killed Frank Tomeski," Clara declared. "He's the one who needs to be arrested."

"Yes, he did!" Stephanie added, her voice shrill with excitement.

Carson laughed, an unpleasant sound that seemed to echo around the hall. "Listen to them. They're completely nuts. Wouldn't surprise me if they killed Tomeski and are trying to blame me." He sent a dark glance at Clara. "If you're so eager to accuse me, where's your proof?"

Dan frowned. "He's right, ladies. You can't go around accusing people—"

Clara didn't let him finish. She held up her cell phone. "Here's your proof. Frank Tomeski was blackmailing Mr. Dexter. They had a fight and Frank lost."

"That's absolutely not true!" Carson turned to Dan. "You're surely not going to believe these crazies? You know me, Dan. You know I wouldn't kill anyone."

Dan's expression suggested otherwise. He held out his hand. "Let me see that."

Clara flipped the phone open and thumbed the button to replay the video. To her utter dismay, the screen was blank. She'd totally forgotten that the hall was darkened. The glare of the footlights had over-exposed the video to nothing more than a white mist.

She looked up to see Stephanie staring at her, eyes wide and questioning. "I'm so sorry," she muttered, "it looks as if—"

She broke off as Carson's voice spoke from the phone, loud and clear. *"Is anybody there?"*

Carson took a step toward her, but Dan stopped him with a burly arm. "Let's just hear the rest of it," he said.

Carson seemed to wilt as the entire conversation replayed from the cell phone in Clara's hand. When it was finished, Dan nodded at Tim. "Cuff him." He turned to stare at Stephanie.

"What in God's name did you do to your face?"

Stephanie grinned, making her look even weirder. "I'm supposed to be a ghost." She nodded at the mayor, whose face was now a mask of resentment. "He thought I was Frank Tomeski's sister, Amy."

Dan shook his head as if giving up trying to understand. He looked at Clara." "You'd better give me that phone."

Clara handed it over.

"I don't know how you gals figured all this out," Dan

said, slipping the phone in his pocket, "but I want you in my office tomorrow to give me a full report. Got it?"

"Got it." Clara glanced at the mayor as he was led down the steps. "It was mostly guesswork actually, and some research on the Internet."

Dan watched his deputy lead the man out the door. "I still can't believe it. After I learned that Stella Wilkins had an ironclad alibi, and then the DNA was discovered, I was so sure it was Sanders. I always thought Carson was a bit shady, but I never would have figured on him being a killer."

"I know." She frowned. "What I don't understand is how you could have found Rick's DNA on Frank Tomeski's clothes."

Dan looked sheepish. "Sanders kept telling me he cut his finger the morning Frank was in his store. He said it had bled on the counter and he thought Frank must have got some on his sleeve when he stole the hammer."

Clara gaped at him. "Of course! I remember seeing the bandage on his finger. If you'd asked me I could have told you that."

He gave her a rueful smile. "Looks like I should have asked you a lot of things. Maybe I should recruit you for the police department."

Clara shook her head. "No, thanks. I've had enough detective work to last me a lifetime. From now on I'll stick to selling books."

"Good thinking. Well, this should solve the case and

put Sanders in the clear." He laid a heavy hand on her shoulder. "Thanks to the both of you."

"And Tatters," Clara reminded him. "Without him, we could have been in a lot of trouble."

"Let that be a lesson to you." Dan patted Tatters' head and started walking away. "You were lucky this time. Better leave the police work to those who know what they're doing."

"Yes, sir!" Clara watched him go, waiting until he'd left before muttering, "If you knew what you were doing, you wouldn't have arrested Rick in the first place."

Stephanie grinned. "Come on, let's go celebrate. Rick will be a free man tonight."

Clara looked at her. "If you don't want to give George a coronary, you'd better go wash off that mess on your face."

Her grin vanished. "Crap. Now I've got some explaining to do." She raised her hands and let them drop. "How the heck do we ever get into these messes?"

Clara shrugged. "Guess we're just in the wrong place at the wrong time."

Stephanie headed for the door, saying over her shoulder, "It sure was exciting, though. Like old times."

From now on, Clara told herself, she'd stick to the new times. It would be a lot safer.

———

She was alone in the bookstore the following afternoon when the doorbell announced a customer. As she looked up, her heart gave a little skip when she saw Rick heading for the counter. "I've been racking my brains," he said, when he reached her, "to figure out a way to thank you and Stephanie for everything you did."

She shook her head. "No need. By the way, Molly helped as well. And Tatters."

He looked surprised. "No kidding. I've got some real good friends."

"Guess you do." He was looking at her again with that gleam in his eyes that always unsettled her, and she quickly dropped her gaze. "So you got everything cleared up at the police station?"

"Yeah, and a pretty hefty apology from Dan. I think he was worried I was going to sue him for false arrest." Rick leaned a hip against the counter and folded his arms. "Can't really say I blame him. The evidence was piling up against me. Even I would have suspected me if I'd been in his shoes. I was figuring on spending a good part of the rest of my life in jail."

Clara shuddered. "It scares me how easily innocent people can be blamed for something they didn't do."

"Well, it's all over now, and I'm looking to celebrate—"

He broke off as the door flew open and a shrill voice declared, "There you are, Rick! I was wondering why you weren't in your store!" Roberta Prince sailed across the floor and came to rest right in front of him. "I'm so happy to see you! I just knew they had the wrong person. How anyone could accuse you of murder is simply beyond me."

Clara coughed, and Roberta threw her a lethal glance before sidling even closer to Rick. "We simply have to go and celebrate, darling. How about tonight? I know this marvelous little place up the coast—"

"Sorry, *darling*," Rick said, in a sarcastic drawl, "but I have plans for tonight."

"Oh." Roberta looked momentarily taken aback, then she quickly recovered. "How about tomorrow night?"

Rick shook his head.

"The next night?"

Again Rick shook his head.

Obviously uncomfortable now, Roberta began to back away. "Ah, well, we can talk about it later. I have to run for now." She hurried to the door. "Good to see you back, Rick." With a flurry of waves she was gone.

Clara watched her stalk past the window and felt sorry for her. Even though Roberta had been readily convinced of Rick's guilt, Clara knew what it felt like to care that much for someone who didn't feel the same way. "She means well," she said, smiling up at Rick. He simply rolled his eyes. "Now, about tonight. I'll figure out some way to thank the others later, but right now I'd like to show my appreciation to you. I was thinking maybe a northern Italian dinner at my place?"

She raised her eyebrows. "You're going to cook?"

"Of course. You haven't lived until you've tasted the fruits of my culinary skills."

"What about Tatters? He helped too, you know."

"I'll save him some leftovers."

She laughed to cover her confusion. It all sounded so intimate. Was she really ready to take the next step with Rick Sanders? Part of her desperately wanted to go, yet another, more sensible part of her was sending warning signals through her head.

Rick was waiting for her answer. She could tell by his expression he was already bracing himself for yet another rejection.

Was it the Quinn Sense warning her, or her own instincts? She decided she didn't care. Raising her chin, she smiled into his eyes. "I'll bring the wine."

NEW FROM ANTHONY AND BARRY AWARDS WINNER

JULIE HYZY

GRACE UNDER PRESSURE

Everyone wants a piece of millionaire Bennett Marshfield, owner of Marshfield Manor, but now it's up to the new curator, Grace Wheaton, and handsome groundskeeper Jack Embers to protect their dear old Marshfield. But to do this, they'll have to investigate a botched Ponzi scheme, some torrid Wheaton family secrets—and sour grapes out for revenge.

KATE KINGSBURY

MANOR HOUSE MYSTERIES

In WWII England, the quiet village of Sitting Marsh is faced with food rations and fear for loved ones. But Elizabeth Hartleigh Compton, lady of the Manor House, stubbornly insists that life must go on. Sitting Marsh residents depend on Elizabeth to make sure things go smoothly, which means everything from sorting out gossip to solving the occasional murder.

A Bicycle Built for Murder

Death Is in the Air

For Whom Death Tolls

Dig Deep for Murder

Paint by Murder

Berried Alive

Fire When Ready

Wedding Rows

An Unmentionable Murder

penguin.com